"E

Beth hurri
comparing. ...ways promised myself I wouldn't stop trusting other men because of him." She blushed. "I guess I have, though."

"You don't know me well enough to trust me," he said.

"We know each other too well for people who met last week," Beth said And she leaned in to kiss his cheek.

He drowned in her scent. Without thinking, he reached for her, turning her face. Her lips were heat and succor and irresistible.

Sighing, she pushed her hands into his hair. She tasted sweeter than hope. His body clamored for more, and he staggered with her in his arms.

When she felt the rail at her back she pushed him away.

"I can't," she said. "Eli... He needs me."

"I need you, too, Beth."

"But for how long?"

Dear Reader,

Sometimes when I'm driving, I see in another car a
family, or maybe a mom and her children, or a dad,
looking harried, staring into the rearview mirror instead
of keeping his eyes on the road. I think how odd it
seems that life in that car is just as vital as my own.
We're all heading somewhere, mixed up in do-or-die
business—or plodding through one day to get to the
next—but we don't have a clue about each other.

I was washing dishes—seeing the first scenes in
Temporary Father—and I thought about those cars.
I wanted to know everything about all the lives in a
small town. So welcome to Honesty, Virginia, where
the houses are quiet, the town is growing, the people
are caring and lives are changing.

A newcomer to Honesty brings heaven and hell to
Beth Tully. She has one priority—getting her son,
who's behaving oddly even for a hormonal preteen,
back into their fire-damaged home. Aidan Nikolas is
recuperating after an unexpected heart attack, which
is attributed to business stress. Secretly he blames it
on guilt over his wife's death. When he meets Beth
and her son, he's struck by need for the optimistic,
hardworking single mom, but he reads all the worst
signs in her son's implacable sadness and sudden bouts
of anger. Aidan cannot walk away from the boy, even as
he tries to persuade Beth she has time to love him, too.

I'd love to hear what you think. You can reach me at
anna@annaadams.net.

Best wishes,

Anna

TEMPORARY FATHER
Anna Adams

TORONTO • NEW YORK • LONDON
AMSTERDAM • PARIS • SYDNEY • HAMBURG
STOCKHOLM • ATHENS • TOKYO • MILAN • MADRID
PRAGUE • WARSAW • BUDAPEST • AUCKLAND

ISBN-13: 978-0-373-71407-0
ISBN-10:   0-373-71407-6

TEMPORARY FATHER

ABOUT THE AUTHOR

Anna Adams wrote her first romance story in wet sand with a stick. The Atlantic Ocean washed that one away, so these days she uses more modern tools to write the kind of stories she loves best—romance that involves everyone in the family—and often the whole community. Love between two people is like the proverbial stone in a lake. The ripples of their feelings spread and contract, bringing all kinds of conflict and "help" from the people who care most about them.

Anna is in the middle of one of those stories, with her own hero of twenty-seven years. From Iceland to Hawaii, and points in between, they've shared their lives with children and family and friends who've become family.

Books by Anna Adams

HARLEQUIN SUPERROMANCE

*The Talbot Twins
**The Calvert Cousin

Mama and Grandpa,
I miss you too much.

CHAPTER ONE

AIDAN NIKOLAS TOSSED his bag onto the bed in the cottage's main bedroom. He stood stock still on the wide-plank floor, breathing in the scent of cinnamon and apple, listening, feeling, believing his heart would beat one more time. And then again and again and again...

He was okay. He rubbed his chest, his left arm. No pain. No shortness of breath. No nausea. Bringing his things in from the car hadn't killed him.

He laughed, with no real humor and certainly without pride. Staying in his friend, Van Haddon's, cottage in the middle of Small-town, U.S.A., also known as Honesty, Virginia, might kill him if he didn't stop dwelling on every flutter of his own pulse.

He shoved his bags across the bed, wrinkling the burgundy comforter. Forget unpacking. He was starving.

After a "minor" myocardial infarction, he'd spent two weeks at home, eating bland pap, living no life, with his parents treating him as if he hadn't run the family business for eight years without their ham-fisted help. A heart attack. At the tender age of forty-two, even though he'd been in such good shape the trainers at his gym left him alone.

When he couldn't stand another second of his parents' tender loving smothering, he'd called Van and asked to borrow his cottage.

The big plan for his first night of freedom? Make some dinner. And listen to the wildlife in the woods of Honesty, population "just under ten thousand." The "just under" must keep them from having to change the sign after each birth.

In the kitchen, a stainless-steel fridge and stove gleamed among granite counters and crystal-clear windowpanes. His box of farm market vegetables and organic groceries looked out of place.

God, this pretty little house closed in on a man.

Despite the chill of a late April night, he flung up the window over the kitchen sink.

It didn't help.

Nothing helped except moving. He unpacked the groceries first. Hard to wait for another pile of steamed veggies, just like the ones they'd plied him with at the hospital. Maybe some "nice apple slices," as the head nurse had suggested, twirling the plate as if it were a kaleidoscope.

Which left him wanting to kill the first cow that crossed his path and eat it raw.

A telephone rang. He followed the sound down

the hall to the living room where the phone lay on its cradle beside a pile of magazines. *Businessweek. Fortune. Business 2.0.*

Aidan touched each cover with reverence. They'd denied him even the *Washington Post* in the hospital. And who knew who'd taken custody of his Treo?

The phone rang again. The old-fashioned receiver had no caller ID. "Hello?"

"Hey. It's Van."

"Thanks for letting me use the cottage." He worked gratitude into his voice. If he hadn't felt so much like a rat in a cage, he would have been grateful. With tall ceilings and cool white walls the living room should have been relaxing.

A faint scent of wood smoke emerged from the cold, blackened fireplace, before which fat couches and chairs squatted around a big square table. A TV sat behind the open doors of an antique armoire that had never been meant for the purpose it served now.

"I'll come down tomorrow and show you the walking paths," Van said.

Aidan stifled an urge to snap that he could find them even after a minor myocardial infarction. "Thanks, but I'll wander until I see them." Then he felt bad. Van, a wunderkind of finance, the one man who always knew which parties to bring to the table, was trying to do him a favor. Aidan dialed back his frustration. "I appreciate your help."

"No problem." Van hesitated. "Have you eaten dinner?"

"I stopped in town for supplies. I'm fine." He wasn't sure he could stand one more pair of watchful eyes, waiting for his heart to explode. There'd been patients in worse shape in the cardiac ICU, but his name and the fame of Nikolas Enterprises had garnered him more interest.

"Come up to the house any time," Van said. "Let me know if I can do anything for you—if anything in the cottage needs work."

Aidan switched on the lamp at his side. Someone had gone to a lot of trouble. Every surface glowed. "Thanks, Van, but it's great down here. See you tomorrow."

He arranged the vegetables on the kitchen counter. Chopping them filled time and made some noise. So did toasting an illegal slice of fresh sourdough bread and slathering it with half a teaspoon of butter. Hunching over the sink, he ate it like a wild dog.

With less enthusiasm, he transferred his piles of celery, snow peas, cabbage, onions and carrots into a shiny silver colander. Next he unearthed a brand-new wok from its box and wrapping, washed it and did a quick stir-fry. Another boring, bland dinner.

He picked up his plate and made the mistake of glancing at the window, where his own face was reflected. And behind him…Madeline. He snapped his head around.

She wasn't there. He knew that, but like a memory come to life, she appeared where he least wanted to see her, when he could least afford to face her.

Just over a year ago, she'd committed suicide. The cardiac team had attributed his heart attack to work pressure. They didn't know guilt drove him or that it was his fault she'd done it.

He set the plate, food and all, in the spotless white sink. Another glance at the window revealed only him. He leaned into the open half, sucking down air, but it wasn't enough. With his mouth gaping like a fish on a riverbank, he headed for the front door.

He pushed it open so hard it swung back at him. The night was colder than he'd thought, cold that bit into his lungs and set a fire that made him cough.

But he didn't collapse. The only band around his chest came from breathing fresh air when he was used to the purified, sanctified, hospital-approved stuff.

He stared into the tall trees, mostly evergreen, waving in the moonlit sky. On the hill above him, Van's house was alight with life. Lamps flickered in glowing pools all the way down to the shrubbery that divided Van's lawn from the cottage's. Another cold breath brought on another choking cough. As he grabbed his chest, he saw movement on the hill.

Someone crashed through the shrubbery, and a woman burst into his borrowed yard, wearing navy sweats, a white tank, holly leaves in her dark-blond ponytail and concern on her delicate face.

"Are you okay?"

He coughed again. It was a defining moment. Not that he was vain, but a lot of women came onto him. Some offered cell numbers and e-mail addresses. More than one had palmed a hotel key card into his hand.

This one, tall and lithe and smelling of pine and exercise, had busted through Van's landscaping, bent on administering CPR.

"I was coughing," he said, seduced by the sheen of sweat on her rounded shoulders.

"Oh." She glanced toward the house. "Are you cooking? Set the place on fire? Van does that all the time."

"I can cook." Now that was an impressive display of testosterone. "I just coughed." Oddly, she didn't produce an oxygen canister. "I'm going for a walk. You must know Van?" He started down the gravel drive, knowing she'd fall into step beside him.

"I'm his sister." She pushed her hand down her thigh and then offered it. "Beth Tully." She looked at him too closely. "And you're Aidan Nikolas."

"Van told you about me?"

Her palm, hot from exercise, warmed his blood. The human contact felt almost too good after night upon night in the sterile confines of the hospital.

"He told me someone was arriving at the cottage today." When she nodded her ponytail licked at either side of her neck. He couldn't help staring. "But I've seen you on magazine covers, too."

Some men might like being one of the sexiest guys alive, but Madeline had chosen to die rather than be with him. He wasn't such a catch. "I try to ignore those. You live with Van?"

"He's taken me and my son in." Not mentioning a husband, she also ducked her head as if she'd said too much. "Our place burned down two months ago."

"That's bad." Great answer. Nice and banal.

She dipped her head again, in a nod. Tall, round of breast, with curves that defined temptation and a voice like the whiskey tones of a forties starlet, she made him hope the husband she hadn't mentioned didn't exist.

"We're rebuilding. It's a fishing lodge."

She stopped as if she'd slammed into a brick wall. Most people filled a silence. Not Beth Tully.

Sick of the sound of his own thoughts, Aidan searched for a way to keep her from running back to her own life. It had nothing to do with her sweet body reminding him he was only forty-two—and that he'd recovered from the heart attack. He was not an invalid.

His wife hadn't wanted him, but that didn't mean he couldn't still want a woman.

"You've lived here all your life, Beth?"

The strands of her hair clung to her neck again. "Except for a year in Florida." Her scent, spice and exotic flowers, drew him even closer. "When I was first married," she said.

He'd resisted those key cards and phone numbers and addresses so clever they'd immediately imprinted themselves on his mind, but he'd never stumbled across a woman so full of life she'd knock down landscaping to save a man. "Your husband lives here, too?" He couldn't help it.

She shook her head.

At the end of the driveway, she turned up the hill. "I'd better get back. My son…isn't Van's responsibility."

Information on that missing husband would require digging. The thought, completely out of character, stopped him in his tracks. "Okay. Nice to meet you."

"You, too. Let us know if you need anything." Gas-lit Victorian lamps helped her up the drive. A sudden thought turned her toward him, and he took a step in her direction. She pressed her fingers to her lips, and then she rammed her hands into the shallow pockets of her sweats. "See you around."

Gravel spurted behind her as she ran up the hill.

What had she almost said?

He'd give a lot to know. He'd give a lot to run at her side. His doctor had insisted on walks at first. Feeling like his great-aunt's favorite old beagle, Aidan lumbered down the hill. He stared at the sky above, mouthing his frustration in words he wouldn't have spoken to Beth Tully.

He'd refused to take the time to see his own cardiologist on the way out of D.C., but he'd agreed to an appointment with a local cardiologist to get rid of the strictures against activity.

And then he could run like that woman. He laughed out loud, and his step lightened.

STILL BREATHING HARD, Beth Haddon Tully climbed white-painted stairs to her brother's porch. Aidan Nikolas. His business deals had skyrocketed Nikolas Enterprises to international prominence after his parents, the founders, had retired.

She almost dropped onto one of the Adirondack chairs that squatted along the sweeping porch. Aidan Nikolas could save her—save her lodge anyway. The bank had turned down her loan application today, and Jonathan Barr, who'd clearly forgotten she was more than the child who'd been his daughter's high school best friend, had let slip the news that he suspected Van would be visiting him for a loan in the near future as well—in the Haddon tradition of trying to save failing family ventures.

Van must be around the house somewhere. He'd returned from a business trip earlier in the afternoon. She ran inside the blue-and-white period Victorian she wouldn't have been able to afford if lottery tickets started flying at her head.

"Van?"

He didn't answer. Beth took off her shoes to keep from spreading dirt or wet grass. Van's housekeeper, the dour Mrs. Carleton, wouldn't approve. "Eli?" Beth's eleven-year-old son had been playing video games, but she'd asked him to take time out for reading before she'd left for her run.

"Hmm?" he said from the living room.

She went to the doorway. Beside Eli, a big, black Lab looked up, thumping her tail at Beth.

"Lucy, girl." Beth ventured into the room and ran a hand over the dog's silky head. "Have you walked her yet?"

"Read? Walk the dog? Anything else I should do?"

"I'll think of plenty." She bent to Lucy, trying not to smile at Eli's tone. After the lodge had burned down, he'd run to his father's house, and he'd been reluctant to come back, claiming he was only a burden to her.

Since then, Eli had been quiet and too cooperative. Bad dreams had begun to plague him. Every time he got up in the middle of the night, Beth heard him. Despite sweat ringing his T-shirt, tears in his eyes and gasping breaths he worked like a grown man to control, he'd never admit something was bothering him.

His simple preteen testiness made Beth want to hug him till he ran from her, screaming like a girl.

"A walk should just about do it," she said. "And it'll be good for both of you. You don't get enough exercise since we moved in with Uncle Van."

"I'd get plenty if we could afford to replace my skateboard."

Already turning toward the stairs, she stopped. "I wish we could," she said, hearing the bank manager's voice from their afternoon meeting.

"I hate to see you struggling," he'd said, "but you didn't even check to see if Campbell had paid that insurance premium after your divorce."

As if she needed reminding her ex-husband was a deadbeat and a liar.

"Mom, I know we don't have the money. I'm sorry I asked."

"It's okay to be mad at me. I hate when you act all grown up."

"It's not okay." He slid off the couch, easing his hand over the dog's head. "Lucy, come."

She scrambled up with a complaining whine. No one in the house felt easy tonight.

"Don't go past the lawn into the woods this late," Beth said, to remind him he was a child.

"Mom." His tone suggested she get off his back.

"I'm serious."

Slamming out of the house, he didn't answer. Beth flipped on the brighter outdoor lights. Taking the stairs two at a time, she ran to the window in her room. Down on the lawn, Lucy jumped on Eli as he cocked his arm to throw her football.

She hadn't ever managed to get the hang of fetch. Eli and Lucy went down in a tangle of gangly legs and black fur and a whippy tail. The ball trickled toward the line of solar lights along the driveway. Eli and Lucy both chased the ball, and Beth reached to close the blinds. Before she pulled the cord, another light caught her eye.

One from the cottage's main bedroom. A golden

glow flooded two wide windows in front of a king-size bed. Not that she could see the bed.

Except in her imagination.

Her mouth went dry. She had no time to be interested in a man.

So many business magazines had splashed Aidan Nikolas on their covers, the late-night talk show hosts had started cracking jokes about him moonlighting as a supermodel—which just proved none of them had seen him close up.

He was handsome enough, but he lacked the vanity. He was just a normal man—who'd looked too long at her and made her uneasy. A shadow passed in front of the windows.

Beth flung herself to the side and then laughed. She stepped straight into view and saw Eli waiting for Lucy who'd moved delicately to the edge of the taller grass.

With a wave at her son who merely set his shoulders, she yanked her blinds and then shucked off her running clothes. She dumped the sweats and tank into the laundry hamper and took a quick shower.

Afterward, she dried, ran a comb through her hair and grabbed her full hamper. In the hall, she walked to the landing and leaned over the stairs. "Are you back, Eli?"

"Yeah." His voice came from behind her. He'd returned to his room—and no doubt to his video games. He was on his spring break. Maybe he deserved time off from chores.

Beth set down her hamper and went to his room. Sweat curled the dirty blond hair that she and Van also shared. The room smelled of boy and dog. Eli barely glanced up.

"Do you have any clothes to wash?"

"In the closet, Mom."

"You could get them for me."

"I'm in the middle of a game. Do you want me to lose?"

"Sounds like a possible tragedy so I'll say no." She held her breath as the closet assaulted her with even earthier smells. "We have to talk about your showering, son." She ducked as a shirt and a coat fell off hangers. They'd been hung so precariously, the sound of her voice had rattled them loose. "And maybe you could tidy up in here before Mrs. Carleton stumbles in and quits on your uncle."

"Hey, Mom, I'm not perfect."

She hardly recognized the mature, strangely guilty voice. "Something wrong?"

"You're bugging me. I'm busy."

She scooped his laundry out of the hamper and then snatched up any clothing near it on the floor. "I'm not bugging you more than usual. What else is up?"

"I'm old enough to decide when to take showers and clean my room."

Maybe he was, but why would that make him look lost instead of arrogant? Where was her son inside those empty eyes? "I wish you'd tell me."

"It's you, Mom, always on my back." He started playing again. If only someone would make truth serum available to mothers. Breach a few civil rights and find out everything you need to know to keep a child safe.

Beth added Eli's things to hers and then maneuvered the whole mess down the back stairs. The laundry room was also part of Mrs. Carleton's empire, but Beth disliked letting the other woman wait on her and Eli.

She turned on the water in the washer and flipped the hamper's contents onto the Formica folding table. Whites. Colors. Cold. Hot. Impossible. The latter pile would include Eli's lucky skateboarding socks.

"Beth?"

Uttering a brief, humiliating scream, she landed safely back on the floor. "Van—do you have to sneak up on me?"

Her brother stood in the doorway, a half-eaten sandwich dangling from his left hand, one of those magazines that loved to cover Aidan Nikolas in his right.

"Isn't it late to start laundry?" he asked.

"Not when I have to work on the lodge tomorrow." She'd put her pennies together to have the charred remains knocked down. Removing it to clear the lot for new construction seemed sure to take her the next year. She pretended to be vitally interested in the clothing so she didn't have to look at him. Should she tell him what Jonathan Barr had said? She was hardly in the position to offer help and he must not want her to know or he'd have mentioned it.

She turned instead to the troubling man who could probably help both of them out of their troubles. "Why didn't you tell me about Aidan Nikolas?"

"I did." He bit into his sandwich.

"You're dropping lettuce on the floor."

"I'm not your son."

"Are we all in bad moods tonight? Mrs. Carleton keeps an immaculate house, and I hate seeing her have to pick up after us."

Van bent down and picked up his lettuce. "I can see why Eli gets fed up."

Taking his shot to heart, she stopped. "You told me someone was coming. You didn't mention my possible deliverance was moving in down the hill." She felt guilty. Aidan had been nice to her. For a second—only a second—she'd been attracted to him. It wasn't polite to think of him in terms of the money he handed out for investment each quarter.

"How'd you find out?"

"I ran into him while I was out." For some reason she didn't admit she'd thought he was dying. Hearing a cough that had sounded more like choking, she'd gone straight through Van's landscaping.

"Something's on your mind, Beth?"

"Salvation," she said.

He studied his sandwich. "Jonathan Barr didn't give you the loan?"

She turned back to her laundry and tossed Eli's blue soccer jersey on top of her underwear.

Barr's voice whispered ingratiatingly in her ear again. "From what I hear, your brother will soon be asking for a loan so we can't count on him to bail you out if you can't repay."

Van didn't want to talk about it. Neither would she.

She shook her head.

"Let me help you," Van said as promptly as if he had no secret need of his own.

"I can't take money from you." Nor could she look at him. She fished the jersey out and put it in the pile with Eli's dark-colored sweatshirts. "I have my own two feet to stand on."

"Why do I have money if not to help my family?"

Touched by the offer of his last dime, she hugged him before she realized he might wonder why. "Thanks, but I can't. You know how it is. Campbell thinks steady work is a bad habit. He's no example to our son. I have to get a business loan from someone who doesn't love me." She piled her jeans and Eli's on the end of the table and then started loading light colors into the wash. "But I was thinking…" She wouldn't be human if she couldn't see safety in a venture capitalist. "Is Aidan Nikolas here to do a deal with you?"

"With me?" He stared at her, and then he looked away. He was hiding something, as surely as Eli. "What could Aidan do for me?"

She watched detergent spin into the water. "Good."

"Good, what?"

"Good that he's not here because of your business." Dark eyes in a pale face floated into her memory. He could save her lodge, with an amount that would be nothing to him. "Jonathan Barr only wants to offer me enough to rebuild the lodge as it was. I told him I wanted to make improvements so that families would come instead of just fishermen. He thinks I won't be able to repay it." She shut the washer lid, trying to hide her frustration. "My typical visitor will continue to be a guy who can't stay long and won't pay much for the bare essentials. I have to get ahead, Van."

He touched her arm. Did she imagine the unease in his eyes? "That's why you're glad Aidan's not here to work with me?"

"I'd like to ask him for—"

"No, Beth. Didn't you see he's been sick?"

"What are you talking about?" His wife had died a year ago. She vaguely remembered that, but the news hadn't mentioned anything about him except his successes. "I have to ask for help." She opened the utility closet and took out a broom to sweep grass that had fallen from Eli's jeans onto the tile floor. "He's my match made in heaven. I need investment. He helps businesses that can't make it on their own."

"He takes those businesses over. He doesn't give people money and expect nothing in return."

"I'll pay him back. You've seen my projections." Her spreadsheets were an inch thick. "What would he want with a lodge in Honesty, Virginia?"

"That was my next question. Any small return you can offer him isn't worth his effort. He looks for profit, not the golden glow of having been generous."

She stared at her brother, hoping he wasn't speaking from experience. "I just have to make him care. It takes devotion to make a business work. And determination. I have both."

Van got a dustpan and held it for her. "When did you start believing in fairy tales?"

"Since my banker let me down. I need a fairy godmother, and don't try to talk me out of it. If he's not here to work with you, you're too late and I'm too desperate."

"He had a heart attack, Beth." Van dumped the dustpan into the wastebasket and took the broom from her. "Aidan came here to recuperate. Do you want to kill him?"

CHAPTER TWO

"KILL HIM? He's in his early forties." Returning to the kitchen, she glanced toward the cottage. "Although he was coughing when I ran into him."

"Coughing?" Van picked up newspapers from the counter and put them in the recycling box. "I never heard of that as a heart attack symptom."

She went to the fridge and took out a bottled water, which she offered her brother. He shook his head so she opened it herself. "No problem, then. I'll call him in the morning and make an appointment to present my business plan."

"No, you won't. He doesn't want his shareholders to know what's happened until he's ready to tell them. He doesn't want the press telling them so I offered him the cottage."

"Are you saying you think I'd call the papers?"

"Beth, listen to me. Don't bother Aidan Nikolas. You are not a woman who can risk another person's health and be okay with it later."

Damn him. "I want to be that woman." She leaned into the back stairs and took a deep breath, using it to make her voice seem normal. "Eli?"

"Okay, Mom—I'll take a shower," he promised in the snarl of a stranger. Uneasily, Beth let his temper pass.

Van gestured toward the second floor. "Is that why you're desperate?"

"He's not himself. He ran away to live with Campbell after the fire, and he's smart enough to sense Campbell was glad when I brought him home."

"You really are scared." With both hands on her shoulders, Van steered her into the family room, switching to big-brother mode. "Tell me exactly what Jonathan Barr said today."

Beth sat on the sofa. In front of her, on a tufted, square ottoman, a pile of towels and linens she'd washed after dinner waited. She picked up a towel, her hands actually shaking.

"I've told you before, you don't have to do laundry."

"And I'm telling you again, I don't love housework, but Mrs. Carleton has enough to do without cleaning up after Eli and me."

Van shook his head. "Why won't you let anyone help you?"

"You mean you? You've helped me all my life. I can do this myself, if someone will just take a chance that I've done my projections correctly."

"But that won't be Jonathan Barr?"

"He said I want too much money and I'm not a good risk."

"His reasoning?"

When he was upset, Van tended to talk to people as if he were querying computer files.

"I should have known Campbell hadn't paid the insurance, and I can't argue with him there. I thought the divorce decree required him to pay it." She took out her anger on the towel, slamming it into folds. "What made me think he'd meet one responsibility?"

"Let me give you the money," Van said. "Eli will never have to know unless you tell him."

"No," she said so sharply Van noticed. She couldn't let him know what Jonathan Barr had divulged. "I can't."

"You won't, and you want me to let you and Eli suffer because you're too proud to take a loan from someone who loves you."

She shook her head, ruefully, to prove it didn't matter when it most definitely did. "Oh, I'm hot for a handout." She folded another towel. "But for Eli, I have to do this the responsible way."

"Pride won't feed you."

"Or clothe us, but you're my brother, not my guardian angel."

She almost asked him if Jonathan Barr had been right, but she stopped herself in time. Van wouldn't tell her the truth. To him, he was still eighteen, and she was ten, and their parents had just died, leaving her his responsibility.

"I'd expect you to pay me back," he said.

"It's not going to happen." Avoiding his gaze, she went for a sheet. There was Eli's father—refusing to take part in raising his own child—and her brother—trying to help when helping might hurt him. She had to consider asking Aidan Nikolas. "What burns me is Barr, talking at me as if I were still in kindergarten. Eight years of making the lodge pay counts for nothing."

"With him. I know you're good for the money."

"Then why do you care if I ask Aidan Nikolas to help?"

"I told you he's here to rest."

"The entrepreneur who runs small businesses with a single thought, chases new opportunities with steel will? The guy who manages to hide his personal life from twenty-first-century paparazzi?" She stood to finish the sheet. "Don't you think he can protect himself?"

Van looked troubled. She tried to remember him before he'd taken the world on his shoulders. First, he'd had to protect her long enough for her to reach adulthood. Then his marriage had ended because of his guilt after his wife had been attacked while he'd been away on a business trip. She'd like to relieve Van of his sense of duty toward her and her son.

"I don't intend to chase the man around his desk—just present my business plan."

"You won't, because it might hurt him."

"I'm not sure I can afford to be noble."

Van's eyes, green like their father's, were so

serious she couldn't look away. "Who are you? And what have you done with my sister?"

She smoothed the edges of one towel. "I'm divorced and a single mom." She started folding another. "I own a lodge that barely qualifies as rubble, and I'm on the edge of bankruptcy. My son is acting odd, and a guy who has money to invest just landed on your doorstep."

Van took a pillowcase off the pile of linens and started to fold it. His silence troubled her more than his warnings.

"Are you sure he's sick? Aidan, I mean? Mr. Nikolas." Her skin felt too warm. She stared at her hands, trying to imagine tall, dark and thriving Aidan Nikolas as an invalid.

Van stood. "It was a minor heart attack, but he's supposed to change the way he lives."

She added another folded towel to the tottering stack, mostly to avoid her brother's watchful eyes. She didn't want to hurt anyone, and she'd sensed a vulnerability that had seemed uncharacteristic in a man like Aidan.

How long had it been since a man had made her want to know anything about him other than his fishing habits? "I don't want to cause more problems for your friend, but I need money."

Van's big-brother frustration covered her like a fog. "If only you'd checked on that policy," he finally choked out—and she realized Jonathan Barr must be right about Van's financial trouble. Van had never made her feel bad about her mistakes. She'd learned at his knee to do what she could to mend and move on.

"Deep down where it doesn't take any effort, Campbell loves his son," Beth said. "How could I guess he'd screw us?"

"He screwed you in every way a man could, and then he started screwing his office manager."

She crossed her arms. She'd felt different talking to Aidan, more feminine, stronger, because someone as responsible and successful as he had been interested. Though she lived with the constant companionship of anxiety and distraction, she was still a woman. She wasn't wrong about the way Aidan had looked at her.

But he didn't know her son was troubled and her business needed financial CPR. Aidan Nikolas wouldn't waste another second of his high-powered life on a woman with her problems. She'd learned that women who made bad decisions had to fight for respect when they tried to start over.

"I don't care what Campbell did."

"If you were a little more honest with Eli, maybe he'd stop running to Campbell and making things worse for himself."

"Honest? I had the man arrested for nonsupport and I turned him into some sort of Robin Hood figure for our son. He thinks Campbell's the victim. Campbell even had him convinced they could have shared that cheesy seventies superstud apartment after the fire if I hadn't dragged him away."

"Let him stay a few weeks and see what happens. Campbell's too busy—" Her brother stopped as if any truth about her ex-husband could still hurt her. "He would have lived off the perks of being a high school football star his whole life if he hadn't gotten you pregnant. He won't want to take care of Eli." Van added the towel that knocked over the pile, which they both restacked into two columns. "Eli's eleven years old. He has to face the truth about his father."

"Not if it makes him more depressed." She stood up to fold a fitted sheet. "How serious is a minor heart attack?"

"Would Aidan let a doctor maroon him in the Virginia countryside if he had a choice?"

"Would he show up just when I need him if I wasn't supposed to—"

"Kill him? A second attack could be massive."

"How long is he staying?"

"You think you're helping if you give him a few days' rest before you send him back to the hospital?"

"I have a doctor's appointment myself tomorrow. While I'm quizzing Brent about what might be wrong with Eli, I'll ask him if offering Aidan Nikolas a business opportunity could kill him."

"I'm sure Brent Jacobs is dying to consult with you on the health of every citizen in Honesty."

She made a face only a brother deserved.

BRIGHT AND EARLY the next morning, Beth dressed and then went downstairs to pour cereal for Eli. Mrs. Carleton called while she was slicing strawberries to say her sister was sick and she'd be in D.C. for the day. Beth left the berries in a sealed container beside Eli's bowl. Then she wrote a note, telling him she'd be back by noon and that the housekeeper wasn't coming.

Even though she'd probably be back before he climbed out of bed.

A quick drive across rolling country lanes, a turn onto a tree-bordered bypass road, and a bridge over the dark green lake that had been part of her livelihood, and she reached town—kind of sleepy on a spring break Monday morning.

The hospital, funded by one of the universities in Washington, D.C., had built towers, like fingers above the trees around the old-town buildings. Her childhood friend, Brent Jacobs, kept an office in one of the complexes connected to the hospital by glass-covered walkways. Beth parked in a lot and hurried to make her early appointment.

In the end, she had to wait. She dove into a cooking magazine. Eli might make it out of bed before she got home after all. A lousy cook, she was trying to soak up instructions for raisin-specked, honey-drizzled bread pudding when she was called to the treatment room.

She recognized one of Brent's colleagues in the room across from hers. And she recognized the man who said, "Come on" with a force Eli could hardly have matched. "Two more weeks? You *gotta* be kidding me."

The receptionist pulled Aidan Nikolas's door closed. "Dr. Vining always forgets to close the door after he looks over results, and heart patients rarely want to hear they have to take it easy a couple more weeks."

Too busy silently swearing to speak, Beth only nodded. She followed the other woman inside and nodded again at instructions to take off her clothing and put on a paper gown.

She couldn't ask a sick man to work on her behalf.

She donned the gown, and for the first time in her life, was too preoccupied to be nervous.

THE LAST PERSON Aidan wanted to see was standing outside a sporting goods shop beside the pharmacy where he had to refill his prescription for beta blockers. He stuffed the medication, bag and all, into his jeans pocket.

"Beth," he said, involuntarily.

She turned, her face flushed, her eyes focusing anywhere but on him. She knew—somehow.

Small towns. Gossip through osmosis.

He moved to stand beside her. "Skateboarding?" he asked, as he studied the colorful boards. "I never realized they didn't come all in one piece." Sets of wheels gleamed as they never would after their first use.

"Me, either, until my son started skating." Beth

lifted her hand to the height of a black board, printed with a bulky, dark green cartoon character in midleap. "This part is the deck."

"Are you buying it? You know you work too much when you don't recognize cartoons."

"I can't affor—" She stopped on a deep breath. "Eli had one something like that before the fire." She looked him up and down and stepped back. "I need to go home."

"Let me take you to lunch." What had she seen? Weakness? Women normally wanted to spend time with him. For once, he'd make time to linger.

"It's barely after eight," she said.

"Oh." His rage at the continued restrictions returned. She followed his hand as he shoved the medicine deeper into his pocket.

"And Eli's on spring break. I scheduled my—an appointment I had—early so I could spend the day with him."

"Okay."

"Come up later, though. Join us for hot dogs or something. Mrs. Carleton—she's Van's housekeeper—she's off today so we're fending for ourselves."

There was a dare in her tone. "I might do that." She couldn't scare him with hot dogs and family fun. He loved the simple stuff.

The frown between her eyebrows told him he'd read her right. "You probably aren't supposed to eat junk food," she said.

He took his hand out of his pocket. "Van told you?"

"About the heart attack." She pushed her finger around the loose collar of her shirt. "He mentioned you'd had a minor problem." She made a huge production of looking at her own watch. "I need to get home. Nice to see you again. Come on up if you get the time. I always make a salad for myself when Van and Eli pig out on the bad stuff."

A MAN—a decent man, no less—had asked her to lunch. By herself. Not because he wanted something from Van, or he taught her rowdy son Social Studies and they needed to brainstorm "solutions" to Eli's behavior.

She'd had to say no. With her heart beating near the back of her throat, she glanced back down the sidewalk. Aidan had already gone. Good.

Thinking he might be attracted was one thing. Feeling attracted to him was exciting because she hadn't cared for any man in—who knew how long?

She'd forgotten the thrill of a caught breath, the tingle of flushing skin, the excitement of a maybe.

But Aidan Nikolas was used to women with no ties except to their clothing bills. She'd already made enough mistakes in her life.

Falling for a handsome, successful man in town only until he felt healthy again would be par for the course for a woman who'd lost her heart and too many years to the captain of the high school football team.

Eli was her responsibility, Eli with his moods

and needs and their lack of a home to call their own. So why had she invited Aidan to join them in a hot-dog fest?

She wiped her palm across her forehead. Had the temperature grown warmer today, or had she backed herself into a hot corner? Lunch would be safe, with Eli and Van to keep an eye on her. Aidan, way out of her league, would see she had other priorities.

She took her phone out of her purse and dialed Van's home number. In a second, her son answered, but she could tell his mind was elsewhere. He must be slaying aliens.

"Hey, buddy," she said.

"Can't talk, Mom."

Alien massacres for sure. "I asked Uncle Van's friend over for lunch, and I wanted to warn you guys. Will you let your uncle know?"

"I'm not sure where he is." His movement made Van's leather sofa grumble. "I think I hear him in his office. He might be on the phone, too. I'll tell him if he comes out."

"Good enough. See you in a little while."

"Okay." He started to hang up. The phone hit the receiver, but then he was talking again. "Mom, did you go by Gross's Sporting Goods?"

Her heart broke. She lied to her son because she couldn't stand telling him no again. "I forgot you wanted me to, son. Maybe we can look together sometime this week."

"It doesn't matter. We can't afford what I want anyway."

She was failing her son, and all avenues of escape seemed to be disappearing. "I'll see you in a few minutes."

"Okay. Mom?"

"Hmmm?"

"Don't worry about it."

She gritted her teeth. "It's normal to be upset you can't have what you want."

"I understand why, though."

Something was wrong. All the more reason not to play sighs-and-smiles with her temporary neighbor.

AIDAN SKIPPED the hot-dog fest. Not that he didn't want hot dogs or another few minutes with the first woman who'd made him feel alive in eighteen months.

At around dinnertime, he'd stood on the weathered gray deck of the cottage, scenting the delicious aroma of a grill at work—wanting to go—but Beth obviously hadn't wanted him to show up.

In the end, he'd lost himself in the business channels on the satellite, pretending that catching up on the news he'd missed was just as much fun. Which probably explained why he'd fallen into a deep sleep on the fat, blue-and-white plaid sofa.

Something thudded into the door a little after six

in the morning. Aidan's eyes opened and he gasped a deep breath. He rolled his head on a sofa cushion, not recognizing the tick of the clock, the rough scratch of the upholstery or the deep, thick silence of no-one-else-at-home.

He'd hardly slept since the heart attack. Not that he was avoiding Madeline's accusing face in his dreams. He did try to sleep.

He pulled on sweats and padded to the front door. Outside, *The Honesty Sentinel* lay on the rug. He picked it up, sliding it out of its plastic sleeve.

His father was the one who'd persuaded the nurses to hide newspapers from him. Aidan had put his foot down the day his mother had tried have his television removed. No CNN? No CNBC? She and his father had retired from running the business eight years ago, but they still kept in touch with the business world.

She was trying so hard to cut him off from it, she must want him dead.

He caught up on the print news of the past ten days, licking his lips every so often in a craving for coffee. The hospital staff had cut him back to one cup a day.

After a caffeine headache that had lasted the first half of his hospital stay, he anticipated the lone, large, rich cup. Every lunchtime, he sipped, making the treat last.

Putting that boon off took all his concentration. He checked his watch. At seven on a Tuesday morning, his mother would be up, also scouting for coffee before she went to the office. He dialed, and a severe British voice answered.

"I'm not sure Mrs. Nikolas is available. May I deliver a message for you to your mother?"

"Tell her she won't avoid my questions about the business by pretending she's asleep."

"Oh, let me have it, Simon." His mother's impatience stabbed at the quiet. "You're supposed to be resting, Aidan."

"What goes on with the Skyliner deal? It's not in the papers."

"How'd you get a newspaper?"

"Mother, I ran Nikolas Enterprises by myself until—" Even the memory of that day made him feel mortal. "Tell me what's happening. Dragonlawn— have they agreed to our terms? I want to start R&D on the redesign of their residential lawn mower. That'll be a quick profit."

"Aidan, I cannot listen to this. Put down the newspaper. Turn off your TV. Lay off the coffee, and go for a walk."

"I haven't touched caffeine, and obviously you haven't, either. Tell me what's going on or I'll browbeat the staff into filling me in."

"You'd have to fire them. Your father and I have warned everyone in the building they're not to worry you about work."

"I'm bored out of my mind." He tightened his grip on the phone. "If somebody doesn't tell me what's happening, I'll fire the whole damn company and start over with loyal associates."

"I'm sure they'll be terrified. God knows I am." His mother turned away from the phone. "Thank you, Simon." She sipped loudly in Aidan's ear. "Ahh, that's better. Look, we're fine. Work's going well. I'll let you know if your empire starts to crumble."

"Let me talk to Dad."

"Sorry. He's already headed to the car."

"Tell him to call me on his cell."

"No."

"No?"

"And I'll tell him not to answer if you call. Between Madeline and a heart attack, we've been on the verge of losing you for the past year. I'm tired of being afraid, and I don't care that you're forty-two. You're still my child. Have a good day, darling."

Aidan pressed his fist to the granite counter. The expensive bag of coffee beans he'd stashed in the cupboard above the fridge sang a siren's song. Bourbon would be even better.

Anything to dull the humiliation. He saw his car keys on the table. There must be a SuperComputer store in town.

They sold laptops.

SMOKE. Eli kept smelling smoke. In his hair, on his shirt and his jeans. Standing in the tall grass at the edge of his uncle's yard, he slapped at his clothes and his head. The smoke followed him like a shadow. It wouldn't leave him alone.

No one else ever noticed because it wasn't real.

He smelled it because he felt guilty—and that scared him bad.

Lucy jumped up, whining as she clawed at his arm. He pointed toward the edge of the lake where the grass grew taller. That shouldn't stop a Lab. "Your ball is over there."

She jumped at his hand instead.

He grabbed her and dropped to his knees, still hugging her. With his head close to her ear, he said it. "I set the fire."

They all thought it was lightning from the storm that day, but Lucy knew the truth. He confessed to her at least once a day, and she loved him anyway. He only half believed she didn't know what he was saying. Telling her made him feel better for a few minutes.

His mom thought he was upset because she'd left his father two years ago. Sure he wanted her and his dad together. Except he could do without the yelling. His dad's yelling—and then the horrible sound of his mom whispering to his father to keep his voice down.

He couldn't figure out why he was always madder at his mom.

Eli buried his face in Lucy's silky ear. She nipped at his hand. She never bit—just held his fingers in her mouth. He burrowed deeper, smelling Lucy and sunshine. He didn't want even her to see him cry.

In the darkness of her fur and his closed eyes, he saw the cigarette again, a white tube with a glowing red top. The blackened match he'd thrown in his garbage can. It must not have been out.

The night before, his mom had been ranting through a news report about kids his age smoking. Sometimes the high school kids came by the lodge and tried to buy cigs. His mother threw them out. She could guess any guy's age.

A lot of kids smoked at the middle school. After his mom had blown up like a maniac, he'd scored one from Billy Thorpe, and then he'd tried it in his room after school.

It had made him throw up. At the time, he'd been grateful for the lightning and hail and thunder that had covered the sounds.

He'd come out of the bathroom to find his room on fire. It had to have been that match. Or the cigarette.

They said a lightning strike had set the fire, but he couldn't remember where he'd left the cigarette.

Sometimes that night happened all over again in his mind. He rubbed his hands as flames jumped at them again. The fire had eaten his blanket when he'd tried to smother it. It had flown across the papers and books on his desk. He hadn't been able to make it stop.

As he'd turned, flames had already started on his DVD player and his video games. Black smoke had wrapped him as fast as he could move. He'd started for the door, but pictured his mom standing out there, waiting to hate him.

He'd jumped out his window, slid across the green tin porch roof and then dropped onto the grass. Trying to hide from another clap of thunder, he'd yelled for his mother and run back inside, where Lucy was barking at the smoke that hovered, waiting to attack from the top of the stairs.

"Get out, get out," his mom had shouted from the landing.

"I can't." He couldn't leave her to fight his mess. He'd gone up and dragged her back down. They'd both hauled Lucy out by her collar.

By the time the fire trucks arrived, they'd all been covered in black soot, he and his mom hugging each other in the rain. Both crying, though she'd never cried before or since.

No one had noticed his burned hands that day. When his mom had grabbed him by both of them the next morning, he'd said he'd burned himself going back for her.

Guilt had made her face different—like she hurt. Maybe that was why something had been chewing on his guts ever since.

CHAPTER THREE

"YOU ASKED AIDAN over here for *hot dogs* and you didn't tell me?"

"Hold it down, Van. Eli will hear that you're upset with me." She laid a piece of salmon on the grill. Mrs. Carleton's sister was still sick and Beth felt safe taking liberties with her kitchen.

"Don't use your son to shut me up. I told you to stay away from Nikolas."

"I didn't say a word about a loan. You're right. I can't ask him for help."

Van opened the fridge and brought back spinach and feta. "You sound upset."

"I am." She shrugged. "He could have been the answer to my prayers. Instead, I'm still looking."

"Are you all talking about that guy in the cottage?"

Beth and Van turned.

"Did you meet him, too, Eli?" Van asked.

"I've seen him going in and out." Eli crossed the kitchen and plucked a grape tomato off the cutting board. "I can see the cottage from my window."

Beth passed him another tomato. "We're supposed to leave him alone. Uncle Van says he's here because he's been sick and he needs quiet to get better."

"I think you should date him, Mom."

"Huh?" Beth turned, and the salmon she'd been in the process of flipping, splatted onto the floor.

"You should date him."

"No, she shouldn't," Van said. "What are you talking about, Eli?"

"I heard you. Mom wants to talk to him. It's time you started dating again, and if he knows you, Uncle Van, he must have the bucks."

"Eli." Beth bent to clean up the salmon. It slipped out of her hands. "Date him? Where's that coming from?" Two tries later, she scooped up the fish and dropped it into the sink.

"I told ya. You need money. He has it. We'd be okay if you went out with someone like that guy."

"We have all the bucks we need, and that's no reason to date anyone. I don't understand you. For the past three years, any time a guy's looked twice at me, you've been upset. When those men who stayed at the lodge left a big tip behind, you thought they were trying to come on to me."

"That was before we found out they tore the mantel off the fireplace in their room." A shrug made him look a decade older. "You need a life, Mom. I feel like a bug under your microscope, and I'm old enough to know you should be interested in guys. I don't expect you and Dad to get back together anymore."

"I'm the one who's supposed to matchmake for you, Eli. You're creeping me out."

"Most divorced moms date. My friends' moms do."

"When the guy is right. And the time. I have to get us back into our own house."

"You worry all the time." He grabbed the plates and silver she'd stacked on the counter. "I'll set the table."

Stunned silence thickened in the kitchen as he rushed to the dining room. Beth turned to Van, still clutching the oily spatula. "That was too many firsts. I should date, I need a life and he's setting the table without being asked."

"He's hiding something. He thinks by going after you, he can keep hiding it." Van popped a tomato into his mouth and turned toward the dining room door. "Sucks to be Eli."

"Wait." She almost lost another piece of salmon. "What are you going to do?"

"Drill for the truth."

"He's been fragile since the fire."

"Which is why I want to know why he's trying to find you a man." Van paused, his hand on the door. "He's been sullen and aloof and he avoids us. None of that is like Eli."

So she wasn't the victim of single-parenting paranoia. "Okay, try, but don't upset him."

"He's my nephew."

She set down the spatula and urged him through

the door. These days she couldn't tell if Eli didn't want to talk to her or just didn't want to talk. They were both lucky Van would step in for Campbell, who grew less paternal as each day passed.

Her brother spoke first. Her son answered. She couldn't tell what they were saying. She leaned on the counter, a knife in one hand, a tomato in the other, trying to hear.

If Van discovered anything earthshaking, he'd tell her. She finished the salmon, mixed greens, tomatoes, feta, almonds and vinaigrette into a salad and hurried into the dining room.

She stopped at the sight of Van and Eli, reading sections of the newspaper. No tantrum from Eli protesting his uncle's nosiness. Nothing but normal.

Normal seemed off.

"Here we go." Crossing behind her son, she lifted both eyebrows at Van, but he shook his head. She set the salad beside Eli and the salmon in the middle of the table. "It's not much for lunch. I should have made rice or something."

"This looks great," Van said.

Eli grunted, which was more like him. Beth scooped up the newspaper and carried it to the kitchen when she went back for drinks. She poured a glass of milk for Eli and tea for Van and her.

Eli followed his usual method—eat, eat and eat some more, until even the salad vanished into distant memory. Then he ran for the front door. He spent every moment of each free day outside with Lucy.

"I forgot to tell him we have to work on the lodge today."

"Leave him here."

"He ought to help. It's his house, too."

"I know." Van stretched to see through the elaborately draped windows. "But Lucy might do him more good than work. I couldn't get anything out of him except what he told us both, but something's wrong. I was sure he wanted you and Campbell back together."

"Me, too." She shuddered. "Don't most children dream of reuniting their parents?"

"That bastard should have gone to jail. He still doesn't pay child support half the time."

"Shh." She glanced toward the door, half expecting Eli to return.

"Beth, listen." Van turned her away from the window.

"Yeah?"

"I have to leave for Chicago tonight. I hate to go during Eli's spring break, especially when he's acting strange."

She wondered if his trip had something to do with his business troubles. "Van, can I just say one thing?"

He nodded, but his eyes didn't fool her. He was worried. "You don't have to protect us. I appreciate your help, but this isn't like with Cassie." Guilt had ruined his marriage, although they'd truly loved each other. "I'm going to be okay, and so is Eli."

"You don't have to assume everything that bothers me leads straight back to Cassie," he said. "You and Eli are my family now."

"It'd be more strange if he weren't acting different. It hasn't been that long since the divorce in child years, and then there was the fire and now he has to get along with standoffish kids at his new school. But please try not to worry. If you don't stop taking care of us, you'll never have time for a family of your own."

"Maybe Eli's right. You do need to date someone. Just don't ask Aidan for help on the lodge."

She wasn't likely to forget seeing Aidan at the doctor's office, enraged because he had to continue taking life easy. "You don't have to worry about that." He'd been wearing jeans and a black sweater that only made him seem longer and leaner. "Not that he makes a convincing invalid."

The doorbell rang. Van glanced that way. "But look in on him once in a while, just in case. I'll be away for a week."

"A fine job for the angel of death," she said, teasing. The bell rang again.

Van kept on stacking plates and silverware, cracking only a small smile at her jab. "I'll do these since you cooked. You can answer the door."

Not one who fought for a chance to wash up, Beth headed for the hall. She opened the front door to find Eli and Lucy facing Aidan Nikolas. Aidan had Lucy by the paw.

"Nice to meet you," he was saying.

"Morning," Beth said, hoping Eli wouldn't notice her voice had dropped low. Forbidden, unattainable fruit tended to take a woman's breath away.

"Hi." Aidan let Lucy go and the dog positioned herself in front of Eli, the picture of canine good manners and protectiveness.

Beth would have preferred to see Eli and Lucy tumbling down the hill with several of his friends. "Come in," she said. "Eli, you met Mr. Nikolas?"

"And I made Lucy shake hands with him."

"Why don't we invite a couple of your buddies over to play? I'm going to work on the lodge, but Uncle Van won't mind, and when I get back we can barbecue."

"No, thanks."

He sounded cheerful, but he hadn't asked to have friends over in weeks. He hadn't visited his buddies in the old neighborhood, either. Before she could say anything else, he patted Lucy's head and spun toward the steps.

"Nice to meet you, Mr. Nikolas. See ya later, Mom." He shot her an encouraging glance that included their guest.

Blushing, she prayed Aidan hadn't seen. Eli had never been impressed with material things—other than a sweet skateboard and the latest cool game. He probably didn't realize his father had come from money until he'd run through it and alienated his own parents.

"Is your brother at home?"

Aidan's voice penetrated. She pried her gaze away from Eli and Lucy. "Van's inside. Come on in."

She led him to the kitchen, where Van turned, dripping suds on the floor. "I'll finish," she said. "Mr. Nikolas—" calling him by his first name was surprisingly difficult "—Aidan wants to speak to you."

"I didn't mean to interrupt." Aidan held out one hand. "I wanted to thank you in person, Van, for letting me use the cottage."

"No problem." Van dried off on a tea towel before he shook his friend's hand and sent Beth a sharp look. She almost laughed after Eli's brow-waggling performance. "Join us up here any time you want. Use the pool—it's heated."

"Thanks." Aidan stopped, and even Beth felt him glance her way.

Van took a step forward, as if to snatch his attention by the throat. "Have you eaten? We still have some salmon."

"No, thanks."

Stiff silence fell. Beth fingered a spot of water off the counter.

"If you're sure," Van said. "Beth tells me you met the other night while she was running."

"She didn't tell you I was choking?"

"Were you?" She pretended to know nothing about his health.

"No, but you burst out of the shrubbery as if you were searching for someone to resuscitate."

"I've recently updated my CPR certificate." Beth tried to laugh off his embarrassment. She might not get men. She might not trust her own instincts where they were concerned, but she was determined to remain kind—even after Campbell. "I thought you might have been Lucy. Every so often she eats her fetch ball and we have to fish the pieces out of her mouth."

"Oh." For the third time in less than five minutes, a man slanted her a knowing glance. Then he turned to Van. "Maybe I will use the pool if you don't mind."

"Any time. Beth's the only one who goes out there. Even Eli won't use it without his friends, and I never seem to find the time."

"Even though you should for your own good." Beth stored the milk and butter in the fridge and wished she hadn't mentioned health. Having seen the proof of his illness in the doctor's office, she thought Aidan looked thin. His hollowed cheeks would only make him more beloved to the photographers, but here in the back of nowhere, they made a woman want to ply him with sandwiches.

"You must get some exercise at the—I believe you said you were rebuilding a fishing lodge?"

"Mmm-hmm. Wouldn't you know it'd burn down when our busiest season is coming?"

"Did you find the magazines I left you?" Van interrupted.

Aidan nodded, but he searched the faces of both

Van and Beth. Undercurrents would be one of his specialties.

"Good. And the television controls?"

"Van, I had a minor heart attack. I won't be needing a home defibrillator or a babysitter."

"Good news." Van maneuvered him toward the kitchen door. "Let me show you the walking trails we've put in."

"I found them."

"Why don't I bring down a couple of steaks for dinner one night?" Van "helped" him through the door, making pathetically sure not to include Beth. As if she'd pitch Aidan over dinner after she'd promised not to. "I'm traveling for the next week, but maybe the week after. Can you eat steak?" Van added.

"Sure."

His short tone made Beth shake her head. She was still shaking it when Van came back.

"He seemed a little annoyed," Van said.

"Can you blame him? You're his friend, but you sounded as if you'd be putting his dinner through a food processor."

"Why are you so defensive on his behalf?"

"I just realized he really was sick and doesn't want to be. No matter what plans Eli has for him, I'm staying out of his way."

BETH CLEANED her room and then slipped into Eli's to tidy the obvious messes—shoes on the dresser, discarded Xbox games scattered in front of the TV and a plate laden with apple pie crumbs.

Then she changed into warmer clothes, tucking a sweatshirt under her arm in case the weather turned chilly. She peered through the pale pink voile over her bedroom windows. Clouds had begun to gather above Van's verdant trees.

She grabbed her sneakers and ran down the stairs. Sitting on the last step, she was tying the laces when the doorbell rang. She hobbled over, one shoe on, one foot crushing a heel, and opened the door to find Aidan cradling Lucy—who was horrifyingly still—and bloody.

Groaning, she tried to gather the dog that was like her second child. Lucy didn't move, but blood from her head smeared Beth's shirt.

"Don't," Aidan said. "That's going to scare Eli."

"Where is he? Please, God, tell me he's not lying out in the woods."

"No, I'm sorry," he said. "I should have told you I saw him come up here. Call him. He'll want to go with us to the vet."

"Eli." She managed a whisper. She'd rather suffer anything than see her son hurt. Couldn't she take Lucy to the vet and come home with reassuring news on her condition? "She is alive?"

"I think someone shot her with a pellet gun. Probably just a graze." As if to back up his diagnosis, Lucy opened her eyes and scrambled for freedom with a whimper that made Beth reach for her again.

Aidan twisted away. "Get your son," he said, his voice harsh with concern.

"Eli." Beth turned toward the stairs. "Lucy's hurt." Great. The delicate approach. Way to destroy a boy. "I'll find him." She stopped halfway up the stairs. "I'm sorry to ask you this, but should you be carrying her?"

A mixture of annoyance and embarrassment chased across his face. "Will you hurry?" he asked, struggling to hold on to Lucy. "She wants down, and she doesn't know me."

On the way to Eli's room, Beth grabbed a couple of beach towels out of the linen closet. She burst through his door, and he yanked out his earbuds.

"What?" he asked, as frightened as she must look.

"Lucy's had an accident." She held out her hands and willed herself to calm down. "Aidan found her. He thinks someone accidentally—hit—her with a pellet gun, but she's going to be okay."

He tore out of the room. She grabbed at his shirt. "Eli, she's bleeding. Try not to be afraid."

"Lucy." He slid down a couple of steps. The dog whined from below. Beth scrambled past Eli on the stairs and this time he held her back. "She's mine. I'll help her."

Beth had no intention of letting him take care of their poor, sweet girl on his own. She reached Aidan first.

"Let's wrap her in these towels and you can sit

with her on the back seat of my car, honey." Using one of the towels, she wiped the dog's forehead, revealing a gash that welled again. "Who the hell was shooting on your uncle's property?" She pressed her cheek to Lucy's ear. "Don't worry, baby."

The dog fought hard to reach Beth. Taking her out of Aidan's arms, Beth let Eli help carry her, stumbling across loose gravel to the car.

He yanked the back door open. "Hurry, Mom."

"Slide across the seat." Together, they eased Lucy in. Beth arranged the towels on Eli's lap, and Lucy laid her head on his thigh. He cuddled her the way Beth used to hold him when he was hurt.

She dug for her keys. Thank God she'd already tucked them into her pocket. She walked straight into Aidan's chest, but he held her off, his hands big, unsettling on her shoulders. "You don't have to come with us." Slipping around him, she hurried to the driver's seat.

"Are you kidding? I have to know if she's all right."

He jumped into the front passenger seat, and Beth hesitated only a moment. She didn't want him to—but Lucy was hurt, and Eli's empty stare in the mirror terrified Beth. She skidded backward through the gravel, but then straightened out to rocket down the driveway.

Aidan hooked his hand into the bar above his window.

"All right, Mom," Eli said. "We'll get you to the doc in no time, Lucy."

"Eli, why don't you get my phone out of my purse and call Dr. Patrick?"

Gently settling Lucy, he leaned forward, but her bag wasn't there. "Where is it?"

She could see it—on the kitchen counter. "At home."

"Mom, your driver's license."

Lucy whined, but more as she did when she couldn't get comfortable on her bed. Beth glanced at her and then back at the road. "You worry too much for one so young, Eli."

"So will the cops," Aidan said.

"You're flying, Mom."

"They can join the parade. Lucy's our girl."

"Yeah." Eli sat back with satisfaction and rubbed his dog's side. She whimpered again and Beth pressed harder on the gas.

She glanced at Aidan. "If you've brought your wallet, you can drive us back."

IN THE VET'S OFFICE, Eli paced awhile, and then Beth wrapped him in one arm and persuaded him to sit. Her fear for him spread around the room in a soft cloud of panic. She tried to be brave and self-sufficient, but her son was her weak spot, and she couldn't hide it.

Aidan stared at his lap. At his hands. Neither vain nor overly modest, he knew he was a capable man. Normally strong as a horse, he wouldn't think twice about taking charge of a last-gasp company or a knock-down, drag-out brawl in one of the pubs where nobody knew his name.

But he hadn't been wise or strong enough to save his wife, and he was tired of fighting grief and guilt.

Eli's distress was familiar to him. It was like looking into a film of his own past.

How many times would he live it all again? His heart still thudded with the disbelief he'd felt as they'd told him about Madeline. Finally, he'd seen the letter they'd pushed into his open palm.

He scrubbed at his hand with the other.

She'd tried so long to tell him she was in trouble, but his idea of help—doctors, meds for her undeniable depression—had all been useless. He'd loved her. He'd held her while she'd cried, and he'd kept repeating he loved her. She'd sworn he didn't even want to be with her.

He'd begged her to come along when he'd traveled, but she'd refused to leave their house.

"Aidan?"

He looked up, his head as heavy as a wrecking ball. He shouldn't like the sound of Beth's voice so much. He hardly knew her, but he'd lost a woman who could fight no longer, and he couldn't help being drawn to Beth's inability to back down from a fight.

"Huh?" he said.

She glanced at the people around them. "Are you—" She stopped as she looked into Eli's curious eyes, but she kept on, lowering her voice. "Are you all right?"

"Fine." He might have preferred she pretend

nothing was wrong with him, but mattering to someone was good—even in a room full of strangers.

In the corner, an older man concentrated on his silent parrot in a cage on his lap. A woman who looked pretty pissed because their dog had gone before her solid, superior cat, sniffed.

"Fine," Aidan said again.

Beth hugged her son. Eli endured her affection, but then shrugged out of her reach, sliding to the farthest edge of his steel-and-orange-vinyl chair.

Aidan read the boy's mind. *Keep your hands off me, but please make this stop hurting.* Again, he made Aidan think of Madeline. She'd needed more affection than he could give unless he held her twenty-four hours a day. And even then…

Eli was desperate and blank all at the same time, need and aloofness that looked too familiar. He shifted his feet.

What was he thinking, really?

That Eli might be in trouble, the way Madeline had been? No one had to warn Aidan he was carrying a masochistic load of guilt, that he might be seeing phantoms. But what if he wasn't wrong?

This family was raw. He couldn't step aside when he saw someone else in trouble. He'd never intruded on anyone's privacy. Too busy. Too smart. Far too comfortable with his own life.

Until Madeline had chosen to die.

He looked at Beth, needing to say her son reminded him of his wife. She walked to the plate-glass windows. A couple of cars whispered past, filled with people caught up in their own errands or pleasure, oblivious to life going on around them.

He loved the idea of oblivion now that he couldn't get any.

Beth took a few circuits around the brick-lined waiting room, and then she sat, far from him and Eli. The lady's cat, two seats away from Beth's new spot, stared at her a second, but then turned, wobbling as it balanced its bulk on four tiny-in-comparison paws, to face the other direction.

Eli paced next, his sneakers squeaking on hard linoleum. He collapsed beside his mother. The cat tightened all its muscles.

"It's my fault, Mom."

"What?"

"Everything." Like her, he ignored the people glancing his way or looking studiously everywhere else.

Beth had eyes only for him. "Lucy's all right."

As she tried to put her arm around him, he pushed away. "Mom." He put "I'm not a baby" into her name. "I shouldn't have left her outside."

Beth leaned into him. "Lucy got hurt in her own fenced yard. She might not have been safe at our place. She might not have been safe inside if someone had shot toward the house."

"Nobody did." He lifted his hand and angled his thumb toward his mouth and bit down.

The world pitched. Madeline had done the same

thing, how many times a day? She'd chewed the skin on the sides of her thumb until it bled. Then she'd start on the other thumb. Aidan's stomach muscles clenched.

"Eli." A force beyond his control dragged the kid's name out of him.

Eli and Beth started and stared as one. This was not the time. Everyone else in the waiting room eyed him.

He looked at Beth's soft face, her lovely half smile that invited him to say what was troubling him.

What jerk would have ever left a woman who could be scared half out of her wits for her child and their dog and yet spare warmth for a stranger who'd just yelled at her son in a vet's waiting room?

He licked dry lips. "Lucy was running in the woods. You had nothing to do with her getting hurt."

Beth's eyes softened even more in a silent thank-you. Eli frowned, and then went on as if Aidan hadn't spoken.

"You know those kids around Uncle Van's house, Mom. They don't have a curfew. They drive their ATVs all over the place. Do you know how many beer cans I've found in the woods? They drink 'em and then they shoot at the cans. They ran out of beer so they shot Lucy."

"No." Beth threw Aidan a distraught look. "Lucy'd hate it if you dragged her into the house every time you came in."

"She'll hate bleeding to death, too. And what about brain damage?"

"She won't have that." Aidan sat on Eli's other side. "And she won't bleed to death. The doctor said a couple of butterflies would fix her up."

Beth looked as miserable as Eli. "Sweetie, let's stick to troubles that make sense. We'll post more signs around Uncle Van's property, but you can't control his neighbors. I'm sorry we had to move across town and you're missing your own friends. I'd be glad to pick them up if you ask them to visit."

"The guys who live where Uncle Van does are snobs. They think they have the right to do anything. It doesn't matter if they kill someone's dog."

"Call your old friends." A hint of tears choked her voice. "It can't be that bad. We've been there two months, and no one's blasted anybody before."

"You don't get it."

"I do," she said, but her son shook his head, and Beth's bigger concern seemed to be calming him down.

"I'm glad you never let me have a gun after all," Eli said.

Beth glanced self-consciously at Aidan. "Firearms have been a bone of contention." She patted Eli's knee, but then linked her hands in her lap. "I was trying to keep you from getting hurt like Lucy."

"It's worse to be the one who didn't get shot."

Aidan stretched his nerveless legs in front of him and hoped the kid would never have any idea how true that was.

"Tell me about it," Beth said.

Eli crossed the room again.

"I don't know what I'm saying wrong."

Aidan held still in case she was talking to herself. He fought an urge to push her hair behind her ear so he could see her averted face.

"That lodge," he said. "Did your husband die in the fire?"

"No." Her glance at Eli was a warning.

"You lost everything?" Had the boy started the fire? Was there something about her ex-husband that shamed her? She looked at Eli, and he stared back. Neither said anything that explained the pointed silence.

"We're starting over literally from scratch," Beth said. Her eyes skated over her son. "But I'm grateful it was just stuff and not people."

Aidan waited. Then, "When will you be up and running?"

"We're having some prob—as soon as I can."

He cracked his knuckles, a nervous habit he'd conquered in sixth grade. "They'll bring Lucy back any second."

"That would help." Beth turned toward the treatment rooms, and her elusive scent floated toward him. She made him uncomfortably aware—starting the moment she'd burst out of her brother's hedge.

He'd climbed into her car this afternoon as if he were the only man on earth who could carry an injured animal. He wanted to be with her, in case he could help. That was what he told himself as he found he couldn't look away.

Even the shape of her lips intrigued him. Part wary smile, part frown. The curve of her throat, marred only by a thudding pulse made him want her and want to protect her all at the same time. He never went for a woman on an attraction-at-first-sight basis.

"Good God," he said under his breath, facing what he'd avoided with all his so-called will. Guilt had nearly killed him, but he wanted Beth because life ran strong and dauntless in her desirable body. Just what he needed.

"Lucy!"

Eli's happy shout startled everyone. The vet led her out by her leash. Underneath a couple of butterfly bandages, someone had shaved the short black fur on her forehead.

Eli slid into Lucy on his knees. She grumbled, but let him nuzzle her head with his. Beth was already beside her son, and they didn't need Aidan.

"Look, Mom. She *is* all right." Eli quizzed the vet with a parental glance. "She is, isn't she?"

"Fine." The doctor ruffled Eli's hair. "I'll ask Chief Berger to send a few patrols by your uncle's house. Maybe put a little fear into anyone who might be shooting in the woods. Since so many animals started turning up hurt, even using a pellet gun is illegal within city limits."

"Thanks." Beth found Aidan with grateful eyes.

"And thank you. For bringing her to us and for coming along."

He laughed, stroking Lucy's fur. "You make me feel like a superhero." Able to stop terrible tragedy by running a dog up a gravel driveway.

"Do you mind seeing Mr. Jingles now, Dr. Patrick?" The lady with the cat marched through Lucy's admiring throng. "He's suffering an excess of hairballs, and you need to tell me why."

She double-timed the doctor back into his examining area. Eli stared after them. "That Mr. Jingles comes by his snotty attitude fair and square."

CHAPTER FOUR

"ELI, DO YOU NEED to talk about anything?" That afternoon, Beth filled her pockets with dog treats and bearded her son in his den. She knelt beside the bed he'd made for Lucy in a corner of his room. Lucy had run for the door the second Beth opened it, but she returned, deeply interested in the dog biscuits Beth set down.

"Mom, you're driving me crazy. What are you, a cop?"

"If you thought something was wrong with Lucy, wouldn't you be like that lady with Mr. Jingles? You'd expect Dr. Patrick to fix things. Right away— not when he got around to it."

"I didn't give birth to Lucy."

He'd recovered his adolescent aloofness. She cursed herself for not striking while he was susceptible. "Is it school? Is someone harassing you?"

"Only in my own bedroom. Go away. I want Lucy to take a nap."

Reluctant to leave, she backed toward the door. At least he was his old self. Nothing bad could happen for a while. "I'll be downstairs, but I have to say one thing. You can talk to me."

His face said it all. *Get out.*

Lucy, crunching the last of her biscuits, gathered her feet beneath her and followed Beth.

"See?" Eli said. "Now she wants more to eat."

"I think that means she feels better." Beth scratched Lucy's back and hurried down the stairs. Eli followed.

Lucy nosed around the kitchen for more biscuits. Eli tried to tempt her with a half-gnawed bone and her squeaky football.

This was more like it.

Unable to resist smiling, Beth found she was like her son. She wanted her wounded loved ones around her. With everyone almost in place, she took her papers out of the desk drawer to peruse her finances again.

"Come on, Lucy." Eli grabbed a couple of biscuits and she crowded him out the porch door. "Here comes Uncle Van, Mom."

He disappeared before Beth could ask where he was going.

Her brother came in, looking back at Eli. "Where have you all been? Where's he going in such a hurry? Did he put something on Lucy's head?"

"He's sick of me questioning him."

"So give him a break." He grabbed water from the fridge. Sweat from running ringed his T-shirt and his forehead. "Where've you been?"

"Someone shot Lucy with a pellet gun. She has two bandages on her head." He hurried back to the door. "You saw she's all right." She looked down at her papers. "Aidan found her in the woods and brought her up. We all took her to Dr. Patrick's office."

"You sure she's all right? What do you mean Aidan went with you?" He turned, the water halfway to his mouth. "What the hell goes on here the second I turn my back?"

"I guess Aidan likes dogs."

"I've never heard that about him."

Beth flipped a page over. What Aidan liked didn't matter. She had a son to care for. Full-time.

"You sure Lucy's okay?"

"Check her out yourself."

He shrugged, set his bottle on the counter and left. In a few minutes, he came back. "Has Eli been hanging around at the cottage?"

"Why?"

"He sang Aidan's praises. I thought he must know him better than a doggie handshake and an emergency trip to the vet."

She sat back. "He didn't say anything to me. I don't want him getting attached to Aidan."

"I don't want either of you hurt."

She smiled. "Cut it out, big brother. I know he's only here for a temporary retreat."

"Good." Van finished off his water. "Not going to the lodge after all?"

"No." She set aside a spreadsheet and rested her chin on one hand. "Eli is so upset I don't want to leave."

"I can look after him." His eyes veered toward the big, old-fashioned clock hanging above the fridge. "I have a few hours before I need to leave."

"Thanks, but I'm staying." She continued, unseeing, to the next spreadsheet. "He won't talk and I wish I could ground him until he comes clean. Maybe I'm hypersensitive because of Lucy." She shuffled her papers in disgust. "It's not as if this stuff's going to change."

"Keep at it, Beth. You'll make things happen."

She stacked her papers, comforted by his faith. Only for a second did she fear it might be misplaced.

"I'm going to shower, and then I have some work, too." He ran up the stairs.

The rest of the day slipped by. Beth tried to pick up the house, but kept straying back to her paperwork. No brilliant idea came to save her or change the bottom line.

Eventually, she set a bowl of water and another couple of biscuits beside Lucy's makeshift bed in Eli's room to help him convince Lucy to sleep with him. The dog usually kept a prone vigil at the front door—where intruders would fall over her.

Beth considered running down to the grocery store for the makings of a cobbler for tomorrow night's dinner—and chicken tenders. Eli loved them.

In the yard, the orange of afternoon seeped into the sky. She searched for her son. "Eli?"

His head popped out of the tall grass where the manicured part of Van's lawn drifted back to nature.

"I'm going to the store. Want to come?"

"No." He dropped again.

"Okay, but go in soon if the grass gets wet."

Beth breathed deep of the fresh air. Such a hard day, but they were all okay now.

HAVING WRESTLED with the new laptop to no avail, Aidan paced through the woods again as afternoon fell to evening. He made no effort to be quiet, bending the branches out of his way, kicking through the pea gravel on the path. Still, Eli's voice stopped him unexpectedly.

At first he didn't understand what he was hearing.

"I wouldn't want to live if something happened to you, Lucy. You're the only one who knows."

Aidan eased closer, making no sound. Eli and his dog lay with their heads touching on the mossy ground beneath the green canopy of trees. Lucy shook her head and her ears flopped, a reassuring doggy sound. Eli must have thought so, too. He rolled over, and pine needles clung to his back. He patted the dog's neck.

"When it's too hard to live, a lot of people decide they don't have to. I'm tired and I'm no good. I almost let you die."

Aidan splayed his hand across his stomach,

almost sick on the spot. Madeline's last, scrawled words screamed at him. *I want to die. You don't want me, and I need you so much I can't breathe.*

Shaking like the half a man he'd been for her, he backed away from Eli Tully. He had to find Beth.

What he'd heard meant getting involved, and that kind of pain was too familiar. He should have been nosy and intrusive and demanded Madeline get the kind of help that would have saved her life.

A man didn't make that mistake twice.

BETH HAD FOUND all of Eli's favorites. Chicken strips, corn on the cob, sweet potatoes to make the soufflé he loved and all the ingredients for his favorite apple cobbler. Not exactly a gourmet combination, but perfect in her son's eyes.

If she'd known how to whistle, she would have given forth with the "1812 Overture" as she dragged the groceries out of her trunk. She hummed instead.

"Beth, I have to talk to you."

She banged her head into the trunk lid. "Aidan— I didn't know you were there."

"Now."

His pale face scared her. "Are you in trouble?"

"Can we go inside?" He reached for her bags, but she drew back.

"You can't carry this. I'll call the doctor."

"Listen to me."

"Where do you hurt?"

"It's Eli."

His tone, totally disengaged, cut straight through her. The bags slipped out of her hands.

Aidan picked up her stuff with robotic determination. "Don't let him see you like this. You have to get him help before he knows you know."

"What's wrong? Stop fooling with those things and tell me where my son is."

As if she were standing outside herself, she wondered at her shrill tone. Aidan kept scooping up the groceries she'd dropped, and then he coaxed her up the porch steps.

He set the groceries on a table in the hall, not noticing when a can of dog food rolled across the cherry surface. He chose an open door and pulled her through, shutting it behind them.

"He's not hurt right now," Aidan said. He let her go and she tried to push past him. His face darkened. "Not physically."

Aidan took her elbows and eased her into a chair. They were in the living room.

She stared at him, half her mind on murder. If she could only get all her body parts working at once. "Where's Eli?"

"I have to tell you some things."

"You look terrible. Something's wrong with you." Something besides a cruel streak.

"I was walking in the woods and I heard Eli talking to Lucy." He explained what Eli had said, but she seemed to hear him on a weird delay, where she understood him about five words after he'd spoken.

"You can't be right."

"I know how you feel. You're tempted to let it go because pretending your son can get better on his own is less frightening than looking a possible suicide in the eye."

She refused to acknowledge that word. "Kids say crazy things when their pets are hurt."

"You're afraid for him. I've felt it since the first time I saw you together."

No one looked that somber without reason. She stood, angry that he should read her mind. "Do you get off on saving the day?"

"I was waiting for you to say something like that. Listen to me. I've been through all the stages."

Fear chilled her. She burrowed into the soft leather chair.

"You want to think I'm wrong because you should have seen if your son was in trouble, and I don't know you well enough to drive when you rush your dog to the vet."

"I hope you're a raving lunatic."

"I *feel* your fear for Eli."

She tried to lick her lips. She couldn't. Her mouth had gone completely dry.

"You can't put your finger on it. You've talked to him, but he acts as if you're the one with the problem."

"You've been eavesdropping—are you a peeping tom?"

"My wife, Madeline, killed herself a little over a year ago."

"No," Beth said. "I knew she died, but—"

Aidan came closer. His body warmth reached out to her. All her blood must have drained somewhere. "I tried to help her, but she thought I was her problem—that I used the doctors and hospitals to get her out of the way."

"Aidan, you must be seeing things." No wonder his features looked honed by every second he'd lived. "That doesn't mean my son—"

"You're absolutely right." He knelt in front of her. "Prove me wrong. Take him to a doctor. Force him to talk. Lock him in a room where he can't hurt himself, but make sure."

Her errant blood rushed back into her brain. She leaned over to still the spinning room.

"I don't want you to live as I do, wishing I'd left Madeline no choice but to get well." Stumbling like a sleepwalker, he went into the hall.

He couldn't be right. It was his guilt talking.

"Eli." She yelled his name, running to the front door, hearing only the too-slow slap of her shoes on the wooden floor. "Eli?"

He and Lucy loped out of the woods. Beth ran to meet him. She pulled him into her arms, finding enough strength to lift her son, whom she hadn't been able to hoist off the ground for over a year.

"Mom, let me go." He flailed for freedom. Thinking she was missing out on a game, Lucy jumped on both of them.

"Stop, Lucy." Beth let Eli go, and the dog fell

back, cowed at her unusual sharpness. Beth stared at her son, aware she was doing everything wrong. "You have to be honest."

"About what, Mom?" Fear entered his eyes. "What did you find?"

"Find?" More important questions pushed his out of her mind. All the times he'd said he was tired, or his "stupid" teachers had given ridiculous homework. His refusal to have friends over and his matchmaking scheme to replace himself. "Are you so upset you'd think of hurting yourself?"

He backed up, tripping in the grass. She grabbed his arm to keep him upright. "What?" He shook her off.

"I heard something that scares me, that maybe you feel as if you didn't want to live."

"Who told you that?"

"I need to know." He wasn't confused. A child should be confused. He stared straight at her. "I want to help you."

"Are you nuts? I'm eleven years old. Why would I kill myself?" He darted around her. "I'm a kid."

She felt as if she were falling. Around her the plants waved their tender heads in earth warmed by early spring sun. Life went on, growing, flourishing, while her world imploded.

An eleven-year-old couldn't claim he was too young to consider suicide unless he'd thought hard about it.

She'd been mooning over Aidan Nikolas when

Eli needed all her attention. She covered her eyes and tried to think.

IT COULDN'T HAPPEN. Not to Eli. Eli wouldn't do that....

She had to do something. If there was even the smallest possibility this was the reason for Eli's troubling behavior, she had to do something.

She tore up the stairs and listened outside Eli's door, afraid to go in, afraid to stay out. Something thumped the door. Something else thudded to the floor. It wasn't Eli, throwing himself around. Even her beloved, injured eleven-year-old boy couldn't move that quickly.

She reached for the doorknob, trying to find words. She'd have to accuse him, and he'd already belittled her suspicions. She'd better find out more than she knew about teenaged boys in this kind of trouble.

Beth went to her room and opened her laptop. Before she reached the Internet, she swore at her own blank-mindedness and reached for the phone.

Brent Jacobs had cared for Eli since the day he was born. When his receptionist, Lisa Franklin, answered, Beth asked to speak to Brent.

"Can I help you, Mrs. Tully?"

"No—please let me talk to him. If he's busy, ask him to call me as soon as he can." She didn't want Eli labeled. Honesty was such a small town—not necessarily filled with small minds—but Eli's teachers probably also used Brent, and gossip sometimes traveled in the guise of concern.

"Hold on." Lisa's annoyance crisped her voice. "I'll see if Brent's in consultation."

A few moments later, she heard Brent: "…wouldn't ask for me if she didn't have a reason." The phone scraped across a hard surface. "Beth? What's up?"

She started crying. The tears surprised her, lodging in her throat and squeezing out of her eyes. "It's Eli."

"Did you say Eli? I can't understand you."

She wrestled for control. "Eli," she said. "I think something really is wrong. It's not just hormones like we talked about the other day."

"You don't mean he's hurt?"

"I'm trying—" To be calm, which was utterly ridiculous. The words spilled out of her. Everything she'd worried about, all the questions he'd palmed off. She ended with Eli's too-adult response to suicide.

"Wait—wait," Brent said. "Bring him in. Lisa, we need an appointment for Eli Tully—yes, I know we were closing, but he's a child and he needs help. We'll stay open for him." He turned back to the receiver. "Beth, our first step is a workup, to see if there's a physical reason for all this."

"Physical?"

"Let's start there. It could be something else, but we'll begin with his physical condition."

"You know what's gone on at our house. The divorce. His father never turning up. His home burning down, me dragging him across town and putting him into a school where the kids formed cliques the first time they saw each other at Mommy and Me classes." She mopped her face with the hem of her shirt. "And he's too late to fit in."

"Be sensible. You're not powerful enough to cause all of Eli's problems. Your first task is to get him into my office because I doubt he'll be glad to come."

"And if that makes it worse?"

"We can't let him decide. Suicide rates for children in his age group keep rising." Brent stopped. "If he gets too upset, tell him I'll come there, but either way, he's having a physical. The worst that could happen is he'll be able to use the certificate for sports this summer."

"Eli's favorite sport is snowboarding. Even this school doesn't make snow so the kids can practice." She switched hands and wiped the sweat off her palm.

He turned away again. "What? Okay. Beth, can you be here at eight-fifteen?"

"Sure." She looked at her watch. "Thanks, Brent."

"No need to thank me. Good luck."

"I'll take all I can get."

She set the phone on her desk and squared her shoulders, preparing to face her own child. What if she drove him to act?

She couldn't think of that. He was more likely to die if she waited and hoped for the best. She went back to his room.

"Eli?"

"Leave me alone. I locked my door."

"Do you know how many times you locked it when you were a baby?" She'd had bobby pins then. She plunged her hands into her hair, finding nothing. Van would have the right tool around here. He must have left for the airport already or he would have come to investigate the commotion.

Eli opened his door and turned his back on her. "I don't want you breaking Uncle Van's house."

"What do you mean?"

"You get some idea in your head and you won't let it go." He sounded a little like his father. Or maybe he was trying to make her mad so she'd leave him alone.

"You and I need to see Dr. Brent. We have an appointment tonight."

Eli stared, his stillness unnerving. "You're nuts."

"I hope so with all my heart."

No emotion flickered in his eyes, but his mouth curved in half a smile. He'd forgotten to change his expression.

"I've been closing my eyes every time I look at you," Beth said.

"Huh?"

"I should have seen sooner. What's hurting you, Eli?"

"Don't talk to me as if I'm a baby. Nothing's wrong, and your old boyfriend, 'Doctor Brent,' isn't going to poke at me."

"My old boyfriend? He's never been that, and he is going to give you a physical if I have to wrestle you all the way to the car and into his office. I'm scared to death of losing you."

"What the hell difference would it make?"

Beth eyed her son, her heartbeat the only sound she could hear. After her parents had died, she'd taken up swearing as a sword and a shield, and Van had despaired. Finally, his unfailing support had convinced her to let go of the anger.

"Losing you would make every difference." Choking on tears, she couldn't finish.

His eyes glittered as he began to cry, too. She didn't know whether to be afraid or relieved. He'd shown so little emotion since she'd made him come home from Campbell's.

"You love me too much," he said. "I don't know if I can live up to that."

She wanted to cry for her son's old, old soul, but she wouldn't. "I don't mean to smother you."

"I'm all you have."

"No, Eli. I have a life—and so do you. You have years to go to the Olympics or become a physicist—or cure cancer. Can't you look forward to them?"

After a steady, staring second, he shook his head and a new flood of tears slid, unheeded, down his face. Beth rocked back and forth on her heels.

"Can I hug you?"

He nodded, and she wrapped her arms around

him. She held him loosely until he grabbed her so tight she wheezed as the air left her lungs.

"Can we go see Dr. Brent?" she asked.

He nodded against her T-shirt. "If you change clothes so no one will see I was crying on you."

"I'll be right back."

In her room, she peeled her shirt over her head and held it to her cheek. She kissed the moist spot where her son had cried. She'd fight hell and all its demons for him. He might as well get used to it.

"MR. NIKOLAS? Can you hear me?" Ron, the IT guy, all but shouted in Aidan's ear.

"Sorry." Focused on the lighted windows up at Van's house, he'd forgotten his top secret help on the phone. "What did I do?"

"You've installed the remote access software incorrectly. I can't see you."

He looked down at his brand-new, so far useless laptop. "It's worse than that. I forgot to hit Return so the machine would log me onto the network."

"You need to do that."

He jabbed the key.

He'd glimpsed Eli and Beth in town. They'd been crossing the parking lot to visit the Honesty Medical Center while he returned to his car from buying the remote login software from the SuperComputer across the street. How long had they stayed? What had they done?

Would that little boy be okay?

Aidan didn't want to care. But who could turn his back on a child?

"Hold on, sir. I'm in." On the monitor, screens began flashing up and down.

"You haven't mentioned doing this for me, have you?"

"No, sir."

"It's not that I'm afraid of my mother."

"I am, sir."

Aidan laughed. It felt odd after so much seriousness. "She can't fire me."

"She'll definitely fire me if anyone tells her or your father I've been setting you up."

"I'll call at night again if I have to speak to you. My parents must have gone home hours ago." The screens kept coming up and closing. "Imagine how you'd feel if you couldn't get to your computer, Ron. You're setting me up to access everything I have at the office?"

"I'll be a few more minutes. When I'm finished, you'll need to change your password."

"I'm making a note." He stood, his cell phone to his ear. Someone passed in front of a window up on the hill. "Ron?"

"Sir?"

"You don't need me to do this?"

"No. I can check everything when I finish because I have your login."

"Thanks."

"Call me back if you have any problems—but don't leave a message."

"No," Aidan said by way of agreement.

"I'll give you my private e-mail. Use that if you need me."

"Thanks," Aidan said. "Seriously." He flipped the phone shut. He was outside before he considered the consequences of butting in again. He climbed the hill before he could stop himself. And he rang the doorbell only as he realized he might be imposing on a family in distress.

Footsteps came down the stairs inside. Aidan slipped the phone he was still holding into his back pocket. Beth opened the door. Her face paled, but she smiled and came out, shutting it at her back.

"I'm glad you came," she said. "I wanted to thank you for telling me about…" She turned around and looked up at the skylight over the door. "But I didn't want to leave Eli alone."

"He's in there?"

"Upstairs, not speaking to me, but he went to the doctor."

"The tests," Aidan said.

"You know about those? How do you survive while you wait for the results?"

He rubbed the back of his head. "I pretended nothing was wrong. I'd do it differently if I had another chance."

"I'm afraid this is my only chance, too, and I don't know what to do." She strangled on her own words. "I'm so afraid."

"Where's Van?"

"He left tonight. Is something wrong at the cottage? Maybe I can help you."

"No, Beth. I came up to see about the two of you. I wish you had Van."

She pressed the heels of her palms to her temples. "Thank you." With new composure, she let her hands fall to her sides. "But I'm sure we'll be fine, and you've already been kind to us."

Kind didn't remotely resemble what he felt, but they were talking intimately because they'd been through similar troubles. "I don't mean to interfere."

"Don't say that. Eli all but admitted something's wrong. He let me take him to the GP." She breathed twice, hard. "Brent—he's our doctor—talked to Eli on his own, but Eli won't tell me what they said, and then Brent told me it was a good thing we saw him. None of that would have happened if you hadn't spoken up."

"I am sorry I scared you and then walked off."

"You were hurt, too. And I don't mind being scared if it means he'll be all right. I'm afraid to leave him alone, but I'm trying to give him room so he knows I trust him."

She seemed smaller tonight, her cheeks softer. He wanted to hold her. "How long did your doctor say you'd have to wait?"

"Until tomorrow. The next day at the most." Startling him, she took his hand in both of hers. "Thank you again. He means everything to me."

Aidan eased his hand free because she was offering gratitude and he needed more. Needed her keenly after living in the strange isolation of Madeline's illness. Physical contact, especially because he wanted Beth without knowing her, without knowing why, made him back away.

"I understand Eli," he said, putting her son between them again. "My father started our company, and as he succeeded, he moved us up the ladder, into nicer houses, with more standoffish neighbors. Eventually, the ones like Mr. Jingles's lady friend, let us know they wanted nothing to do with our new money."

"Your father was probably trying to give you a better life than he had."

"I'm not complaining, but I've been where Eli is, and it felt as if summer would never come."

"Every year?" She moved to the porch rail and sat.

"Every year," he said. "Until I made myself popular—with a Harley and a really cool boat."

Beth's confidence returned in a smile that started his heart pumping overtime.

"I'd rather he was sure of himself instead. I barely managed to replace his video games and my laptop. Van gave Eli one of his old ones."

"Weren't you insured?" That information was none of his business. He could tell by the change in her wide eyes.

"That's a long story, and my son and I have

already mired you in our problems." She pushed her hands down her legs, not knowing she made him ache to follow the slow, graceful progress of her fingers over the curves of her thighs. "Do you want a beer?" she asked.

"A beer?"

"You know, to drink?"

"Sure. No one said I couldn't."

"But maybe alcohol is off limits until your doctor tells you it isn't." She looked him over as if everything that had happened during his hospital stay was written on him.

"I'll take that beer."

"I'll get two." She stopped at the front door and looked back, holding it open. "Why are you doing this?"

"Drinking a beer with you?" He knew exactly what she meant.

"Why do you keep helping us?"

"Eli reminded me of Madeline, and I couldn't walk away."

She caught his sleeve. Her touch disturbed him, even with the thin material between them. "Eli's father isn't like you. Not that I'm comparing," she said in a hurry. "But I've always promised myself I wouldn't let Campbell stop me from trusting other people. Other men." She blushed. "I guess I have stopped, though."

"You don't know me well enough to trust me," he said.

Beth's eyes invited him closer. Her smile made him wonder how soft her lips would feel. It wasn't serious, this wanting her. He'd recuperate—same as he'd get over the heart attack.

"We know each other too well for people who met last week," Beth said. And she leaned in and kissed his cheek.

He drowned in her scent. Without thinking, he reached for her. One hand splayed over her back, seeking warmth. With the other, he cupped her chin and turned her face. Her lips were heat and succor and irresistible.

He kissed her once, and leaned back, long enough to see a flash of green in her startled eyes. Then he lowered his head again, taking her mouth without hiding his need.

Sighing, she pushed her hands into his hair. Her mouth opened. She tasted sweeter than hope. So hungry and passionate his legs felt heavy. His body clamored for more, and he staggered with her in his arms, until they reached the rail.

As soon as she felt his arousal, she sprang back. Her mouth still open, still moist.

"I was trying to thank you," she said. "That wasn't thank you."

"I didn't know I wanted you so much."

She slid her hair off her shoulders, and he liked watching the play of her fingers on her neck.

He crossed his legs.

"I can't," she said. "Eli—he needs me."

"I need you, too, Beth."

"But for how long?"

"What?"

She wrapped her arms around her waist. "Any woman hates asking, but I'm a mom whose boy is in trouble. I have to ask, and you have no answer."

Her bleak expression hurt. He pushed away from the rail and walked down the steps. Behind him, the door opened and closed.

CHAPTER FIVE

"How long?" she'd asked as if she had any right, as if it weren't one of the scariest questions anyone could ask. And the man had only kissed her.

Had she lost her cotton-picking mind? Campbell always said she wanted to be in charge. She'd have loved feeling as if he were taking care of her, but he'd never been capable.

Now she had to wonder if he was right. *How long?* Still shivering with the memory of Aidan's potent caresses, she buried her head in the papers that had become her talisman. She might be losing her business, but those figures would turn into her lifeline when she found the perfect combination of numbers to suit a banker.

Eli and the numbers. She had to keep them foremost in her mind.

Upstairs, something tumbled across the floor of Eli's room. Lucy barked her playful yap, and Beth sighed in relief. No doubt they were playing catch with Lucy's chunky football.

Beth stared at the ceiling. She'd half considered

not bothering to tell Campbell about the trouble with Eli. He'd think she was imagining things. But if Campbell was with Eli when something like this happened and didn't tell her, she might just kill him.

She climbed the stairs to her bedroom and dialed his number from her cell phone. It took her three calls before he picked up, though he always swore he didn't ignore her.

"What is it, Beth?"

"Eli." She told him everything. Campbell said nothing when she finished.

"Are you still there?"

"What are you doing to my son?"

Naturally. "I'm trying to take care of him."

"You're determined to make him need you. Leave him alone and let him have a life. You don't want him to grow up and be a man."

"That's exactly what I do want." She turned her head toward the door. Could Eli hear her through it? "What is the matter with you, Campbell?"

"I'm not paying for this. It's a figment of your imagination. He's perfectly all right."

"I didn't ask you to pay for anything. Don't worry. I don't expect you to help with your own child anymore. Were you ever the man I thought you were?"

"What about you? Did you ever hear of having fun? Eli would be fine if you'd let him have a little."

"Fun for me is seeing him clothed with a roof over his head. Fun is knowing he's safe."

"Let's not start this again. I think Eli's okay. You think he's a nut, fine. I won't have anything to do with it."

"Campbell, if you say anything like that to him, I'll… I don't know what I'll do, but you leave him alone."

She pushed the End button. Had she been blind at sixteen?

She thought of Aidan, kissing her senseless, making her feel more than Campbell ever had. It meant nothing, compared to her feelings for Eli. She had her eyes wide open now.

ON WEDNESDAY, Beth woke early and started breakfast. She called Eli only once before he clattered down the stairs, an anxious Lucy at his side.

"You okay?" Beth asked as they sped past her to get outside.

"Mom."

She took that as a yes, but she stayed at the door as he and Lucy ran toward the woods. She'd planned a full schedule for the lodge today.

Work, to occupy his thoughts and his hands. That had been her grandmother's philosophy. Beth had been seven when her grandma had taught her to embroider. She'd learned knitting at eight, and by then, she could clean a house to her grandmother's exacting standards. Mope or misbehave at Grandma's and you'd find yourself manning a mop.

She'd died about a month before the car crash

that had taken Beth and Van's parents. Back then, it had seemed like the worst thing Beth would ever have to endure.

Lucy and Eli emerged from the woods and raced back to the house. Beth jumped out of Lucy's way.

"I think she's hungry," Eli said. "She only ate those biscuits yesterday."

The dog was already lapping water when Beth ladled beaten eggs for omelets into her favorite pan. "I have to clean up in here before Mrs. Carleton shows up." She consulted the clock. "We don't have much time."

"She's scary." Eli buzzed out of the room. "I'd better check the hall. Lucy ran through some mud."

Was he as happy as he sounded? Would she ever accept anything he did without a second thought again? "I thought we'd work at the lodge today," she said.

He didn't answer until he came back to the kitchen, his face knotted. "Mom, it's my spring break." He went into the pantry and came out bearing the bag of Lucy's expensive, but very good-for-her kibble. "I'll go along, though."

He'd better believe he would. "For?" She added sautéed onions and mushrooms and a few green peppers for Eli.

"What do you mean?"

"You'll go with me, but you don't want to help me clean?"

"That place stinks, and I'm supposed to be on

vacation. Harrison Damon's family went to Tuscany for spring break."

"Tuscany? Wow—you think the Damons would adopt us?" Eli wasn't lazy. No saint—she didn't fool herself—but he'd never ducked a messy job before.

"Ben Leitner's going to Disney World."

"Along with sports stars everywhere."

"Huh?"

"Don't they show those commercials anymore?"

"You're not listening." Lucy, in front of him, whined and shuffled her feet, clattering her nails.

Beth peeked at the bottom of the omelet. "What do you want to do?"

"Find out if the other guys are skating. You're the one who always says I don't get to see the kids from my old school."

God knew cleaning knocked-down walls and waterlogged Sheetrock and their ruined belongings depressed her enough, and he'd already run away once. "I've had all the big stuff taken out. We can hand carry everything else that's left."

"Are you afraid to leave me alone?"

Lucy scratched his leg with a paw and he scooped a tin cup full of kibble into her bowl.

"I could lie, but I am afraid. I don't want to leave you alone until we understand what's making you sad."

"I'm not going to hurt myself, Mom."

"Last night, I read some stuff online. You may

not want to do anything like that, but sometimes children feel so desperate, they do things they can't ever take back."

"So you're going to sit on me until you're sure I'm not desperate?"

"Not sit on you exactly. Let's call this work therapy because I love you so much I can hardly think about anything else." She didn't mean to add to the pressure, but what if he needed to hear she loved him?

He gave Lucy another scoop and then wrestled the kibble back into the pantry. "Mom, you're making me mad."

"I don't blame you."

"Like with that. Pretending to be reasonable." He looked plenty mad, with his hair on end and his eyes crinkled in a scowl that was starting to look familiar. Who knew how long his pain had festered?

"I'm fighting for you, Eli."

"Fighting for me? Don't be a drama queen." He softened as she backed up a step. "I just want to see my friends. I hate going into the lodge the way it is now." He scooped his thick hair off his forehead. "Maybe I should go live with Dad."

Fat chance of that. What had once been her worst fear didn't seem so frightening now. "You could ask, but you won't get free rein at his house, either." If she was lucky, Campbell would just ignore Eli's calls and not spread his version of the truth about her worries. The last thing Eli needed was Campbell's treatment plan.

"I'm not hungry," her son said.

He slammed the pristine white pantry door on his way down the hall. She opened her mouth to call him, but waited, the spatula in her hand. Didn't he deserve the right to fight back?

Only his own strength would save him in the end. Chewing on the inside of her jaw to keep her mouth shut, she picked up the omelet pan and dumped breakfast down the garbage disposal.

Why couldn't she run the world and make everything right for her family? Was it so much to ask?

"DAD, I've got a problem."

"What's that, son?"

Score. An excellent start. Sometimes when Eli called, his father didn't have time to talk. He'd ask if he could call back, but then forget. Eli jumped into the opening. "Mom took me to the doctor."

"You have sniffles? You know your mom—she panics over every little thing. Just buck up and be a man. Put up with her crazy ideas a little longer, and soon you'll be on your own."

Uh-oh—the "out on your own" speech. Eli switched phone hands and rubbed his palm down the side of his leg. "Dr. Brent did all kinds of tests." Maybe that would get his dad's attention.

"Doctors must panic, too. You're not really sick?"

"That's what I'm trying to tell you. Mom says I'm depressed, but my only problem is, I don't want to live here anymore. I don't like Uncle Van's house."

"Is he mean to you? He never liked me, either, buddy. It's just a little while until your mom gets some money to fix up the old place."

"What if she doesn't? The bank didn't want to help her." He'd looked into that file she kept in the kitchen desk after she'd started lying to him about money stuff.

"Van will help her. He has plenty in the bank."

His father sounded a little jealous. Eli shrugged to get the creepy feeling off his neck. "Dad, can I come live with you?"

No answer. Something ran into the wall in the hall, and Eli jumped. He came out of his room, hiding the portable phone behind his back, but Lucy, who'd apparently felt she had an appointment with him, scrambled to her feet and ran through the door. Even the floors around here were too ritzy for him and his dog. She always slid on the wax. He'd bumped into Mrs. Carleton more than once on her hands and knees trying to polish out the scratches from Lucy's paws.

Lucy ran to her pillow and nosed around until she found one of yesterday's biscuits. Eli lifted the phone to his ear again and shut the door.

His father still wasn't talking. Eli's stomach flipped like he'd driven off the track on a video car game.

"Dad, are you there?"

"We tried living together right after the fire. Your mom didn't like it. I can't help it if she doesn't want you to live with me full-time. Like I say, we have to put up with her craziness." He whistled, to imply birds circling around her head.

Eli tried not to get mad. "We can fix it. She doesn't like you leaving me alone most of the night, and she says you never fix me anything except popcorn and TV dinners." He pushed his hand across his chest. His heart was going so fast it scared him. He'd never said anything like that to his dad. He might never let him visit now. "If you'd try a little harder, I could stay with you more."

"She doesn't understand us men, does she?" His father didn't seem to be mad. Eli stared at the phone. Was it cutting out? Hadn't he heard what Eli had said?

"I can make her let me stay with you, Dad. Just come get me and promise you'll make the kind of food she does."

"I'd like to, but the timing sucks. You know how much I want you with me, but I've got a line on a job over in Maryland, and I'm not sure how often I'll be home. Like I say, son, suck it up. Be a man."

All right. This time Eli was mad. His mom on one side, questioning him like a cop, and his dad on the other, never hearing a word he said.

"Dad, I *am* a man. You don't have to keep telling me to be one, but I don't like to live here. Mom's on me like I stole her car or something. I don't like the kids at my school, and I'm sick of the lodge. Let me come stay with you."

"Can't do it, son. Wish I could, but you call me whenever you want to talk, and we'll have another nice get-together like this on the phone. I have to go now, but I love you, Eli."

He felt sick as his chance to escape slid away. "I love you, too, Dad, but I wish you'd let me come."

Eli sat in the floor and leaned on Lucy. Why couldn't his mom be friends with his father? Naturally he didn't want Eli visiting for more than a weekend when his mom always had to act like she was in charge of both of them. Like his father didn't know anything about kids. His dad was used to pretending nothing was wrong.

He stared at the phone in his hand and then threw it across the room. It marked the wall with a black scrape.

Eli grinned.

BETH TIPTOED down the stairs. She eased the front door open and slipped through, closing it behind her without making the slightest whisper. She ran off the porch and around to the back—out of Eli's view from his windows. She'd been afraid he'd catch her listening after he threw the phone against his wall.

That bastard. She shouldn't have eavesdropped, wouldn't have if she could be sure her son were okay, but Eli, saying "Dad" again and again had stopped her.

What was the matter with Campbell? Couldn't he tell Eli wasn't himself? His idiot "be a man" mantra.

Funny coming from a guy with a barely passing acquaintance with the concepts of manhood.

She wanted to hit something. To shake sense into her ex-husband, to hug her son until he realized he could count on her no matter what.

She squeezed her temples between her hands and then let go with a groan. She'd do Eli no good hanging around the back of her brother's house, wringing her hands like some soap opera diva.

She marched inside to make a new omelet, which she took upstairs with a glass of chocolate milk and a chewy bone for Lucy.

"Hey, you two. Look what I have."

"Mom, did you listen when I was on the phone?"

Lying came like second nature. "Did you call someone?"

He'd picked up the phone and was eyeing it as if it might bite him.

"You always tell me not to eavesdrop."

"I was cooking. See?" She set the tray in front of him and then fished the bone for Lucy out of her back pocket, wounding herself in the process. "Here, girl." She flipped the bone onto the sleeping bag cum dog bed, and Lucy pounced on it. Beth rubbed her ears.

"I'm not hungry," Eli said in a reflex response, but he smiled as Lucy growled around her bone.

"Try a bite. After you finish, we'll head over to the lodge." She shook her head as he started to argue. "No, wait. Maybe you should call and see if any of your friends can play." She leaned down and kissed the top of his head. For once she thought he leaned toward her. "I love you."

"Maybe I'll call Jeff Lockwood."

"Good idea. He has an extra skateboard, doesn't he?"

"Can we go over to the parking lot at the Food Trader?"

"You know they don't like you guys skating over there."

"Mom, I'm going to be in the Olympics one day, snowboarding. This is the only way to practice when it's not winter." He forked a bite of egg into his mouth. "Besides, I'm a man. I can decide what I want to do."

With a helpless nod she tried to walk—not wobble in rage—into the hall. "I'll be downstairs when you're ready."

"Okay. You're sure I can go to Jeff's? You're not just tricking me?"

"I may be overprotective, but I'm not dishonest."

"Sorry, Mom."

As soon as he turned on the shower, she dialed the bank. The receptionist offered help with her usual enthusiasm.

"This is Beth Tully. May I speak with Jonathan Barr?"

The woman connected her. "Beth, what's new with you today?" Mr. Barr asked.

Normally, his "let's be friends" tone annoyed

her. "Nothing's new, except I've found a little common sense. I'd like to come talk to you about an amount the bank would lend me."

"We can do that. When will you come in? I'm pretty full today, but tomorrow at eight-forty-five, I have an open half hour."

"I'll be there." She forced down a bitter lump of humiliation. "I don't know how to thank you, Mr. Barr."

AFTER ELI PROMISED not to skateboard at the Food Trader, Beth dropped him off at the Lockwoods'. In sweatpants and a ponytail and a dusting of flour, Jeff's mom came out to the car.

"Hey, Beth—how's it going?"

"Fine, Ann. Are you sure both boys won't be too much trouble?"

"I'm glad you let Eli come." She waved him toward the knot of children fighting over big yellow toys in her yard. "He keeps my offspring occupied. You know how little ones look up to older ones."

"I've heard." Beth would have loved another child, but that chance seemed to be passing her by.

"Don't kid yourself. They say two are as easy as one, but they lie. Two is twice the work. Three, three times and, let me tell you, with four, I'm lucky if I remember their names and don't put Jeff in Kailyn's tutu before I send him off to Jamie's cello lesson."

"You make it sound good." That was chaos she'd love.

"How much longer before you can start rebuilding? I can't believe you've done most of the cleanup yourself."

"I hired help for anything toxic and for the appliances and the bigger stuff, but I've mostly got shove-the-rest-of-the-trash-into-a-Dumpster duties from now on." She leaned her head against the seat. "After two months, I can't wait."

"I'll bet." Ann reached in and squeezed her shoulder. "We'll be glad to have you home, too."

Jeff and Eli ran toward Ann's minivan. Beth grabbed her friend's hand. "Where are you taking the boys?"

"Over to that new half-pipe they put up in the mall, but I don't know where they think they're going. I'm not ready yet."

"A half-pipe? In the mall?"

"They installed it over a weekend. Jeff's been there almost every free minute since, and the other children and I play on the kiddy equipment until they get tired enough to shout encouragement at their brother."

"Sounds like fun. I'm missing out on all these days with Eli. You'll stay with them, won't you? You won't leave the boys alone when you get to the mall?"

"I don't make that mistake since Jeff was a show-and-tell example at kindergarten. Police Officer Chris used him to explain what happens when little children wander off. Speaking of cops, I heard what happened with Lucy."

"I know. Can you believe people being so reckless? Nothing like that ever happened here. Who told you?"

"Trey." Ann's husband was a fireman, but several police volunteered part-time in Honesty's fire department and provided a conduit for talk about town happenings. "Dr. Patrick got the men all worked up. No one likes to see a pet hurt." She glanced back toward the boys. "I'd better gather up the troops. See you later, Beth."

"Thanks for the chat. I'm losing touch with my own life."

"You're just too busy to check in with the old gang." Another squeeze of the shoulder, and Ann was off, chasing her toddler daughter who veered out of the garage, carrying a diaper and her dress.

Normal problems. Ann was a lucky woman.

Beth waved goodbye to Eli, who wore a big grin as he rocked back and forth on Jeff's skateboard. In a few minutes she turned down the long, narrow lane that led to her house. The woods here were older than at Van's, fuller. The lake seemed darker. Fish were plentiful and swimming free, instead of being sacrificed to her guests.

On the last curve in the road, Beth dodged a truck filled with teens front and back. There was barely room for two vehicles. The road had been carved out of wilderness during Honesty's horse-and-buggy days.

Beth glanced in the rearview. Kids kept breaking

into her garage and storage buildings to indulge in their vices. She didn't want anyone getting hurt in her derelict ruins, and she sure didn't want to end up on the bad end of an affronted parent's lawsuit.

She parked down the steep hill from the lodge and started to go up, but the dark water called to her. She'd dreamed beside it, imagined a clean, honest future for Eli and herself. She walked down the deck, taking her time, breathing in honeysuckle and a hint of wood smoke.

From another deck on the far shore, her friend, Les Kyle waved. He rented boats for a living, and his business had been off since hers had burned to the ground.

She waved back and then faced what was left of her house. It had once nestled like a Christmas card into Virginia evergreens. Now a pile of rubble, it looked like the cover of an old gothic novel. All she needed was a long-haired girl in her nightgown fleeing from the burned pile etched into the tree line.

After checking the outbuildings for vandalism, she took coveralls and a mask from her trunk and climbed the stone steps set into the hill. Donning her work things, she chanted her own mantra—just a few more days of this—and with the help of the loan, she could start rebuilding.

The acrid smell of loss burned her lungs. She opened the garage and got out her wheelbarrow and then rolled it back to the rubble. The house had burned all the way to the porch. This had been her domain, her way out of debts left from her marriage.

Her success had grown with each passing month since she'd asked Campbell to leave. She'd felt it crackling in the tips of her fingers every time she'd run her end-of-month spreadsheets. It hadn't been just bad wiring and an old computer. She'd felt the future, sparkling within her reach.

Not just for her, but for Eli. She'd liked going out, no longer having to worry that Campbell would cause a scene. She'd drifted to sleep each night secure that she was showing Eli how hard work provided for their family.

She pulled on her gloves and grabbed a hunk of waterlogged drywall. She was tipping her third wheelbarrow into the Dumpster at the edge of the porch when she heard a truck coming.

She looked up, wary that those children had come back, but it was Trey Lockwood. A couple more men from the neighborhood sat beside him on the front seat. Behind them, four guys shouted from an open Jeep.

Beth set the wheelbarrow on its rests. She couldn't yell back and the men blurred in front of her eyes. Grinning as if he'd brought Santa and the Easter Bunny and Cupid on Valentine's Day, Trey presented his work crew.

"Ann said we should bring you home faster," he said. "So I rounded up everyone who was off duty today. Where do we start?"

"Are you sure? I don't know how to ask…"

"You don't have to."

Beth took the hint. "It's pretty nasty in there. Do you have gloves? I have extra masks in case the air's bad."

They'd brought their own gloves. Each man took one of the masks she stored in her trunk, and everyone pitched in. On her next trip to the Dumpster, Beth found herself behind Trey.

"Thanks," she said as he veered around her.

"My pleasure. We should have thought of it before." He actually looked embarrassed.

"Listen." She cocked her head toward the pile behind her. "They're laughing. I've had to keep my mind blank to keep doing this work."

Trey almost rubbed her shoulder, but stopped when he saw the soot on his gloves. "It's not our house, Beth. You think any one of us wouldn't be in bad shape if this happened? I don't know how many times we've talked about teaching that bastard ex-husband of yours to face his responsibilities."

His quiet-spoken anger spooked her. "Lending me all these hands is much more useful."

CHAPTER SIX

THE COOL MORNING AIR gave way to growing heat as the sun climbed toward the middle of the sky. Beth had forgotten to bring lunch. She glanced at the men, lining up to dump garbage from whatever they'd found to use as scoops. They must be even hungrier. She'd had wheels to push her loads to the Dumpster.

She was shaking her glove off to check the time on her watch when another vehicle came down the lane. Not a truck this time. Maybe Ann had brought the children and lunch in her minivan.

It wasn't Ann. Beth recognized the car that emerged from the trees, and she couldn't have been more startled. She glanced at the men who'd helped her all morning. Friends, every one, they felt like brothers today.

How was she going to introduce Aidan?

He got out of his car, bearing a sack printed with a picture of a small cabin. Trust a friend of Van's to bring takeaway from Uncle Moe's, the disarmingly named, most expensive restaurant in town.

His smile grew serious as he realized he hadn't brought enough for everyone.

Beth hurried down the porch steps. The others just stared. "How did you find me?" she asked.

"I asked where your lodge was." He lifted the bag. "At Uncle Moe's."

"I'm sorry—that was a rude way to thank you." She sensed the other men coming in the way his glance slid around her.

"I'd better go back for more," he said.

"I can't ask you—" She wasn't even sure why he'd brought food for her.

"You didn't," he said, paraphrasing Trey. "You really have been doing this all by yourself."

"Until today. These guys are my neighbors." She stepped back. "Ted, Trey, Ben, Lyle, Gary, Rick and Jim, this is—" She stopped again, her mouth going dry as she remembered those moments in his arms. She stared at his mouth, his firm, disturbing seductive mouth that had turned her into a woman she hardly knew. She couldn't say his name.

"I'm Aidan Nikolas." His intimate look unsettled her. "A friend of Beth's."

The other men darted curious glances at her, but they stepped forward to shake hands, each shucking off a glove. None seemed to catch on to the idea that Aidan was a minor celebrity.

Maybe none of them cared.

"If you'll let me write down what you'd like, I'd

be glad to get lunch for everyone," Aidan said. No one turned him down.

"Arthur's, about a half a block north of Uncle Moe's has the best burgers in this part of the country," Trey said.

"I could do with one of those myself. Same for everyone?" The men all nodded and so did Aidan. "Do you want to come, Beth?"

"I couldn't leave everyone else working," she said and ignored all the laughing suggestions that she was being too polite. "But thanks, Aidan. I never expected…" She didn't know what to think. Bringing meals for a lot of strangers went above and beyond a guy wanting a kiss.

"I'll be back."

THAT NIGHT THEY FINISHED before the sky was more orange than blue and the evening chill set in, although Beth suspected it would take a blizzard to make her feel cool tonight.

After delivering lunch, Aidan had rented a small trailer and brought out wheelbarrows for everyone. He hadn't pitched in, and he'd matter-of-factly told the other men why. Laughing, he'd offered to be the team water boy, apparently more willing to risk discovery than look like a slacker. Beth had a feeling these men had bonded. None of Aidan's new friends would divulge a word about him.

Even though she moved away whenever he came near, Beth felt proud to know him by the time the other guys shoved their wheelbarrows back into the trailer. Trey shook his hand with approval.

"I'd never have guessed a guy like you could let down his guard." He looked at Beth. "You've been a good friend to her. Hope you stay well, man."

"You did know." Beth could tell by his tone.

He flicked an imaginary straw of hay from the side of his soot-darkened mouth. "We ain't all rubes, ma'am."

She punched his arm. "Idiot. Van made me think I shouldn't be spreading information about you," she said to Aidan.

"You know how the papers are. They'd turn a minor heart attack into an incurable illness. I'm following doctor's orders even when they humiliate me, but I won't lie about my own name, even for the company."

"You're safe with us," Gary said.

"But maybe you should try an alias," Trey said. "See what you can get away with. You sure can't do it when you grow up in a small town that just gets smaller because everyone knows you. That Van, Beth. He wasn't always such a stuffed shirt."

She laughed with the others, but guardedly. He was her brother after all.

Jim tossed his gloves into the Dumpster. "I'll talk to my brother-in-law tonight and have him get in touch with you tomorrow, Beth. First thing to do is pour the foundation and then look at the framing." His brother-in-law was a contractor in the next town.

"Thanks, Jim, but I have an arrangement with

Sam Grove. He said I could let him know with a few days' warning." Of course, he also wanted money. She looked from man to man to man. "I seem to have thanked you all several times, but I don't know what else to say."

"You'd do the same for us," Rick said. "Ann was right. We should have been over here before now."

With tired good-nights, they trooped down the hill to their cars. Aidan took out the keys to his rented trailer.

"I'd better get that back. Know anyone who needs six wheelbarrows?"

"You bought them?"

"I couldn't find a place to rent them."

"Aidan, you shouldn't have."

"I brought wheelbarrows and lunch. It doesn't mean anything."

What did it mean that he looked at her as if kissing her was still on his mind? How no one else had noticed...

"Where's Eli?" he asked.

"Playing with Trey's son. They're best friends."

"That's good medicine." Aidan pointedly ignored her confusion. "Why don't we pick up some dinner? What do you think he'd like?"

"Why?" Beth asked, refusing to pretend that kiss hadn't happened.

"Why pick up dinner? I'm starving, and you probably are, too. If Eli's been playing all afternoon, he's hungry, and we're neighbors."

"It has nothing to do with what happened last night? You have no other motive?"

Aidan flipped the rental keys in his hand. "I thought over what you said—what you asked."

"Please don't mention that. I literally burn with shame."

"It must have been hard, and I understand why, but I don't want things to be uncomfortable between us."

How could they be anything else? She still had him on her mind, too.

"I was trying to tell you I'm Eli's mom first, and he's in trouble right now. Maybe that kiss meant nothing to you." Even she didn't believe something so powerful could have been innocuous—even for a man like him.

"Don't pretend, Beth. You know it mattered to me. I think you have time for Eli and me. I don't want to say give us a chance, but I do want to bring you dinner."

She'd be crazy to risk it, but he lifted a curl of her hair, and as he tucked the strands behind her ear, his finger brushed her lobe, and she shivered, head to toe.

"Eli loves pizza," Beth said in a thick voice. "Smothered in pepperoni. I'll pick him up and we'll meet you at Van's house." She plucked at the blackened T-shirt that rose above her coveralls. "I'm not fit to dine with."

"I disagree. Think we should have some wine?"

"Okay, if it's all right for you."

He went down the hill ahead of her.

She peeled off her coveralls as Aidan tried and then tried again to back out his trailer, grinding gears. He waved sheepishly as he finally straightened out.

He didn't have to worry about looking masculine. His kindness and faint self-consciousness, his ability to laugh at himself, and his prickly acknowledgment of the restrictions that held him back made him man enough.

"YOU WERE HELPING Mom?" Eli asked around a mouthful of pepperoni.

Beth would have suggested he chew first, but she was too happy seeing him interested.

"I was a total loss as help," Aidan said, sipping Kool-Aid. The grocery store beside the pizzeria hadn't sold wine. He lifted the cup in admiration. "This stuff's pretty good. Like sangria without the kick."

It was nothing like that, but Eli laughed and Beth eased deeper into the cushion on Van's kitchen banquette. She'd showered and made her arrangements with Sam Grove about the foundation before Aidan had arrived with the pizza.

Now she was propped with one elbow on the table. She'd sleep well tonight. The lodge site was clean— as it could be—and her friends were still her friends.

"What did you do?" Eli asked. "Mom said you helped."

Aidan shook his head. "Here, Beth, eat something before you fall asleep." He put a piece of pizza next to the crust she'd left from her first slice. "Your mother doesn't ask much. I passed around water bottles."

"And magically made equipment appear. And he brought us food and picked up everything we dropped." She lifted the pizza. "Which you shouldn't have done, Aidan."

"I'm alive." He sounded as smug as if he'd tricked the universe.

"I could have done that," Eli said. He eyed Aidan as if he were seeing him differently. "I should have."

Time for a quick change of subject. "How did your skateboarding go?"

"I learned to do a grab."

"Is that where you hang on to the board while you ride it?"

"Yeah. It was so cool—like flying."

She hated to think of her son dangling in air. "Wow," she said. "Did Jeff teach you?"

Eli nodded. "He's better than I am since he's been practicing, but I'll catch up." He poked Beth's drooping hand. "You are falling asleep at the table, Mom."

She'd taught him better manners. "Sorry." She dropped the pizza before it landed in her lap. "I'm too tired to chew."

"Go to bed," Aidan said. "Eli promised to show me his new video game."

She tried to smile, but it wouldn't come. She glanced at Eli. "Do you mind cleaning up, honey?"

"Sure." He started scooping up the paper plates and plastic cups they'd used. "Even I can do this without driving Mrs. Carleton crazy."

As soon as the kitchen door shut behind him, Beth turned to Aidan. "What are you doing?"

"Nothing."

"Why pretend you want to know my son?"

"Pretend?" He pushed back from the table. "I want to know you both."

She didn't speak.

"Your rules," he said.

"Rules?" She woke up then. "You're not going to hurt Eli."

"No." He looked horrified. "What did your ex-husband do to you? As soon as I get close, you think I'm the kind of man he is?"

"You don't know anything about him."

"You forget what a small town this is, and the kind of resources I have. I know about Campbell Tully."

She closed her eyes for a humiliated second. "I don't think you're like him, but I don't want you to be Eli's friend for a while and then disappear."

"I won't."

"Why? He can't get attached to another part-timer."

Aidan leaned across the table, his elbow squeaking on the polished surface. "If I could walk away, I wouldn't have told you what he said to Lucy. I am involved."

"But will Eli have any say in deciding when you aren't anymore?"

He came back before Aidan could answer. "I'll go get the game. He can stay, can't he, Mom? It's not a school night."

Beth stared from her son's eager face to Aidan, frowning as if he resented her. Her need for control came from deep inside. She'd only managed to escape Campbell and his reckless debts and his refusal to be a parent because she'd taken control of her own life.

But she didn't want to hurt her son by controlling the people he could talk to.

"Eli promised to teach me all about driving cars in a galaxy where gravity does not exist." Aidan had softened his tone. "I just bought a new computer, and I may need a game, myself."

Beth touched her son's hair. He slid out from under her hand. "Sounds like fun," she said. "How about if I watch you play?"

"I'll bring my laptop down to the family room." Eli disappeared, settling the matter.

"Please be careful," Beth said without looking at Aidan.

"He's a good kid. You don't have to act like this."

"I know." She did know, really. It was just remembering that overheard phone call with Campbell and how dangerous it could be if Eli was unhappy right now. "We'd better watch him set up the game. He's an impatient teacher."

Aidan held the door to the hall for her. "I'm not

good with games. I use the same software all the time for work."

"You'll get it. It's easy," Eli said.

"I'll check the kitchen. Mrs. Carleton will be here in the morning." Beth went and wiped down the counters, steeling herself to act normally.

She'd once been arrogant enough to believe living with Campbell hadn't affected her opinion of other men. She'd been wrong.

When she went to the family room, she found her son and Aidan sitting in front of the soft, wide ottoman Van used as a coffee table. Eli had his joystick and he was dancing with it, driving his car in unknown star systems.

"Whoa," he shouted. "That Taxwinian hit my fuel tanks or I'd have made it. You think you can do it, Aidan?"

"Maybe." The man grinned and looked good enough to make real magazine models weep.

Beth avoided his dark gaze and curled up on the sofa across from them. Again, manners would have suggested she sit up, but lack of willpower defeated her. In a little while Eli's victory shout woke her. She must have fallen asleep.

Despite all her worst fears, she liked having Aidan near. It was one night, but she glimpsed the blessed safety of sharing worry and watching her son have fun with a responsible male.

Her eyes drifted shut. She tried to open them. But eventually gave up, not knowing she had.

Later, she woke to feel something soft sliding across her arms. She lifted her head, but Aidan's voice shushed, and Eli choked off a laugh. Aidan's hand lingered on her shoulders, as he smoothed a soft, warm blanket around her. In a dream world this wasn't only one night.

Eli whispered good-night. Without even meaning to, she'd left her son in someone else's care.

"MRS. TULLY?"

Beth opened her eyes. Armed with a duster and disapproval, Mrs. Carleton loomed above her. Beth moved her hands and found she was on the sofa, swathed in a woven blanket. Morning had come. Sometime during the night, Eli and Aidan had left her.

"Mrs. Carleton?"

"Where's your son?"

Beth sprang to her feet. "I don't even know what I'm doing here," she said and wondered why she was stopping to explain.

She ran through the house. She and Eli had both fallen asleep on couches before, but neither of them walked off and left the other. Eli had told her once that knowing she was in her bedroom at night made him feel everything was okay. He liked structure.

So what had happened?

He'd been happy last night. Had something changed?

Some message on his computer? Had something Aidan said upset Eli?

Too scared to call her own son, she pounded up the stairs and stopped at his open door. He'd made his bed.

Or he hadn't slept in it.

"Eli?" Back downstairs she hustled.

"Mrs. Tully," said the housekeeper, trying to stop her by the door. "Are you all right? Have you tried the cottage?"

The cottage? The words barely made sense.

She ran down the porch stairs and nearly fell as she leapt onto the gravel. "Eli." She had to stop. Get a grip.

The sound of laughter stopped her in midstride on the driveway. It came again from the cottage, and she caught her breath as she tried to look calm.

Aidan and Eli were sitting in rockers on the porch. Lucy, at their feet, thumped her tail, but they didn't notice. Eli took a portable video game player from Aidan's outstretched hand. "You're getting good. You're better than my mom. She starts laughing because she drives too fast, and then she falls off the track."

"Maybe she only plays to hang out with you."

"You don't know my mother. She looks like she thinks about nothing but mom stuff, and she pretends to be even tougher than she is, but she loves to win. She'll beat you at anything." Eli pointed to the screen. "You were going too fast, too."

"I wasn't thinking."

"You like her, don't you?"

"Eli." Beth cut in, not wanting to hear Aidan's answer. Both man and boy raised their heads—with very different looks on their faces.

The warmth of awareness washed over Beth's body. She liked being wanted. Last night had changed something between her small family and Aidan.

It scared her more because he'd chosen to bring dinner. He'd chosen to play with Eli. He'd tucked her in with a familiarity she wished could have been real.

He'd leave Honesty as soon as his doctors let him.

She turned to Eli. "You should have told me you were leaving the house."

"You were asleep. We left you on the couch 'cause you were so tired, so I didn't want to wake you up." He grinned. "I'll bet Mrs. Carleton didn't like finding you this morning. We saw her drive up."

"She wondered where you were."

"I bet." Eli looked at Aidan. "She's my uncle's scary housekeeper."

"She was concerned I'd lost my son."

"That's not my fault. This is spring break, Mom. I'm taking a vacation at home this year."

"So you keep saying." At least he was cheerful. "Let's get some breakfast. Mr. Nikolas is supposed to be taking care of himself, and I'm pretty sure his medical team never advised him to spend a morning listening to you yell at your game."

"He only yells when he wins," Aidan said. "I'd yell, too. I never realized these things were so hard."

"Can you believe he's never played them?" Eli asked with a piteous look at his new friend.

"He didn't get to where he is by burying his brain in a toy." She should have run her fatherless-in-every-way-that-counted son straight home, but Beth was compelled to point out that a busy man could be as happy as one who worked equally hard at not having business at all.

Despite her elephantine subtlety, Eli stared as if she'd started spouting Latin.

"Come on," she said. "You need food."

"I had grapes."

"I'm thinking yogurt and a banana? Maybe some oatmeal."

"Are you serious?"

Good food had to be good for him. Healthy fuel would prepare him to face an unsettled world. Or so her grandmother would have suggested.

"Sleeping on a couch doesn't make me sane in the morning. Let's find a compromise."

Eli stood and Aidan handed him his game. "You wanna come, Aidan? Did you eat yet?"

After a brief look at her, Aidan shook his head. "Can't," he said with real regret. "I have things to do around here now that my laptop's working."

Eli looked disappointed, but he thumped down

the stairs, Lucy at his heels. Behind him, Aidan stood and braced one hand on the porch stanchion. "What goes on at the lodge today?"

"As long as the rain holds off, they're pouring my foundation." And she had to face Jonathan Barr, who acted as if he printed up the money himself.

She tugged Eli's arm. "We'll see you later, Aidan. Let me know if you need anything."

There. She'd done Van's bidding, too.

She didn't look back. "Eli, you can't run down the hill the second you wake up in the morning. Aidan's a busy man."

"He wanted to play, Mom."

"Did he tell you that?"

"He didn't have to. I brought the game downstairs last night when we got tired of using the computer, but the batteries wore out. I found new ones this morning."

"New ones?"

"In Uncle Van's remote."

She tried not to smile. "You shouldn't raid Uncle Van's things, either."

"I like playing a game with someone else instead of by myself."

"But Aidan has a job and he's busy getting well." And he might leave her boy, just as Eli's father kept doing.

"He doesn't mind, Mom." Eli turned his game on again. "I can tell. I know when someone's bored and doesn't want me around."

If she didn't destroy Campbell Tully with her bare hands, she'd deserve canonization. Two deep breaths brought her voice under control. "He still has work to do. You can't go over there without asking me. He won't be here long, you know."

"Yeah, I know."

The buttons clacked on his game and circus-type music pealed from the gizmo.

"Why don't you and I play after breakfast?"

"You're not very good, Mom."

She must have looked scared again. Or maybe sad. He grabbed a corner of her shirt. "You could be better," he said. "But you worry about me beating you and your hands don't move fast enough."

"Eli." Might as well be blunt. He deserved honesty. "I'm going to tell you why I'm out of sorts this morning. I don't want you to get attached to Aidan Nikolas and then have him leave."

Eli moved away from her. "You can't pick my friends, and you can't run my life."

HE REFUSED TO TALK after their brief, harsh exchange. Mrs. Carleton agreed to look after him while Beth kept her appointment at the bank.

Beth felt as if everyone in town was staring at her as she got out of her car. A few blocks away, the courthouse clock tolled the half hour. She'd arrived early.

She was eager. Mr. Barr's assistant, Libby showed her in with a smile of greeting. The loan officer had already fanned out her paperwork on the desk in front of him.

"Join me." He waved at the captain's chair across the scarred conference table. "Lib, a cup of coffee for Mrs. Tully. Sit down," he said, patting the other side of the table as if she were still sixteen.

She almost said no, feeling too beholden and anxious, but the cup would give her something to do with her shaking hands. She sat, screaming a silent plea at every power in creation to get this over with. She needed so much more than the bank would give.

"Don't be nervous, honey. We'll finish this and the money will be yours."

Not enough. Never enough. She'd end up borrowing from Van and being ashamed of herself, praying she wouldn't shame Eli, too.

"I'm so glad you came to your senses."

For a second, she imagined throwing the loan papers into the air between them. She couldn't afford pride, so she swallowed her temper.

"Eli needs his home back," she said, not caring what he thought. "So I'm settling for what I can get."

He pushed the top paper across the desk. "Here's what I can offer."

She hid her dismay. Mr. Barr waited, expectant, ready for gratitude. "It could have been worse," she said.

"See? I knew you'd think straight again. You were always a smart girl—"

He broke off so sharply it was as if she'd heard him add "until you slept with that no-good Campbell Tully."

Going to the bank had become an exercise in humility. She didn't like being called a girl or "honey." She knew without being reminded what a blunder she'd made marrying Campbell, but Eli was no mistake. And she couldn't tell Jonathan Barr off as he deserved if she wanted her house back.

"Where do I sign?"

"I've marked each line with red arrows."

"Thanks."

Lib came back with coffee that churned acid in Beth's stomach before she even touched it. She searched the documents for red arrows and signed so fast no one would ever recognize her name.

"Shall I give you a certified check? Or I can transfer this amount into your account."

It was easier to see him as some cruel loan shark rather than the bank's reliable employee, but none of this was Mr. Barr's fault—except for his chauvinistic attitude.

"You can deposit it."

At last she turned the sheaf of papers toward him. He tapped their edges, arranging them and smiled as if he were Midas, gilding her in honest-to-God gold. "Just pay it back on time, and next time I'll be able to give you better terms."

Rage kept her silent. She might not choose to deal with him next time, but rebuilding the lodge meant she had to take the loan and the check in silence. "Thanks, Mr. Barr."

Somehow, he'd managed to signal Libby. In a few minutes she came in with a receipt showing that the money had been deposited in Beth's account.

"Here you go, Beth. I'm glad to see you getting on your feet again."

She took the receipt for a loan that would actually get her as far as her knees. "Thank you" went through her mind, but she'd never know if she managed to utter the words.

She stopped at one of the high, glass-topped tables in the lobby and wrote another check, to Sam Grove's company.

With any luck, he'd be able to send out a crew this afternoon or tomorrow. Sam had promised they'd pour the foundation over the weekend at the latest. That was the kind of new start she needed.

CHAPTER SEVEN

SAM WORKED at the edge of town from a Quonset hut set in the middle of a gravel yard. She negotiated a path through the heavy equipment and found him in the office—tall, running a harried hand through his dark brown hair, answering a phone and talking to one of his men all at the same time.

He waved her inside. When her turn came for his attention, he shut the door. "I wish I could lock this," he said. "Silence. Don't you love the sound?"

"I've had more than my fair share." She pulled the check out of her back pocket and unfolded it. "I have the money."

He took the check without looking at it and dropped it into the drawer of a gray metal desk he then locked. "I think I can get a guy over to your place in the morning. If we pour the foundation in less time than I estimated, I'll cut you a break on the cost."

"Thanks, Sam. I won't pretend every penny doesn't matter."

"Like with everyone. I hear you and the guys in

your neighborhood made short work of the last of your debris yesterday."

"Yeah. Thanks to them, we finished way ahead of schedule."

"Gary and Jim suggested I should pour the foundation for free."

"No." Her sharp tone made him draw up his eyebrows. "I should jump at the chance, but I don't want charity." She looked down, twisting her hands together. Sam had also known her since kindergarten. She didn't have to tell him why she cared so much.

"Campbell Tully was an idiot back then and he must lose more brain cells every day. Believe me, there was a time when I thought you and Van acted too good for all of us and you needed a lesson in real life. But Campbell Tully—I wouldn't leave my dog in his care."

"He wasn't always—"

"Beth, most guys can't be the captain of the school football team for the rest of their lives. Usually, they grow out of the disappointment."

"You're right. Maybe I was as naive as everyone says, but I only want him to be a good father to our son now."

She'd never been this honest with Van. Suddenly, between Aidan, Mr. Barr and her old friends, she was offering an oral journal on her private life, one entry at a time, all over town.

"Campbell has nothing to do with this, Sam. I'll meet you out at the lodge tomorrow?"

"We should be there about the time the sun comes up. I'd like to finish in one day."

"Only a magician could extract Eli from his bed at that hour. I may be a little later—unless you need me?"

"We'll just about manage." He barely hid a laugh.

Beth laughed, too. Unlike Jonathan Barr, he condescended kindly. "Eli and I will be over early."

"See you there. Maybe I'll let Eli drop a load of cement."

"That'd make his day."

ON HER WAY HOME, Beth's cell phone rang. With dread and hope, she read Brent's office name and number on the screen as she pulled over. Brent himself answered her hello.

"We have the tests," he said. "I can put your mind at ease about physiological reasons for Eli's problems, but we need to go the counseling route next. I have three names I can suggest. People in town, and I trust them."

"You'd take your child to them?"

"Absolutely."

Too late, she remembered he and his wife had been trying to have children for several years. "I'm sorry, Brent…."

"Don't worry, Beth. It was a figure of speech. Let's talk about Eli."

She dug for the small pencil and a piece of paper she'd started keeping in her pocket soon after she'd opened the lodge. The only way to keep track of guests' favorites. "Can I have the names?"

He read them off, along with phone numbers. "I think you and Eli should talk to all of them. See who fits best. Why don't I let them know you'll be calling?"

"Thanks, Brent."

"I'm glad you brought him to me so early."

"Do you want to see him again?"

"Not unless you think his physical health is being compromised. And of course, if he wants to talk…"

"I may take you up on that. Let me see how he reacts to the idea of counseling."

"I'm always here. I've told the staff to put you through to me unless I'm in the middle of an emergency."

She'd made some bad choices in her life, but moving home to Honesty just before Eli was born hadn't been one of them. "Thanks, Brent. You make me feel safer."

But only as long as they were talking. The second she hung up the phone, she became a single mother—panicking.

THOUSANDS OF E-MAILS HAD stacked up while he'd been out. Aidan did a quick crap scan and deleted the chain mails, jokes and anything else that required a waste of his time.

He'd have to do another cull later, but he started over at the beginning and tried to catch up on his business.

God, it felt good. He made a mental note to reward Ron in IT with a big bonus.

Working in the silent house took some getting used to. Instead of basking in efficient lighting, his laptop glowed in a cloudy afternoon that spread shadows across the dark wood floor and fat, plaid furniture.

Instead of the whisper of voices and keyboards and the varied rings of cell phones up and down the halls, his only accompaniment was a grandfather clock, slowly ticking in the corner of the open dining room.

After a while, he found himself staring at the screen, seeing nothing. Despite his need for work, he couldn't seem to concentrate.

That couldn't be the heart attack. He glanced through the windows, twisting in the chair to see Van's house. It was too early in the day for lights, but a faint glow issued from between curtains in an upstairs bedroom.

No doubt Eli's. Aidan stood. The garage doors were open and empty. Van had left his at the airport. Beth must be out. Mrs. Carleton would be with Eli.

Still, he worried. He hardly knew the boy, but Eli mattered. He started for the door, but stopped himself. He was reacting to Madeline's death, not to Eli's behavior.

And how many times would Beth let him butt into their lives? He was trying to persuade a woman incapable of asking for help that she could trust him. She could even imagine him walking out on a boy who needed a father figure.

She refused to see he was trying to build a normal relationship with them both. Aidan pushed through the door and started for one of the walking trails instead of the house. He headed downhill with momentum that brought up his heart rate.

Without warning, Beth bolted from behind a bush growing across the trail, straight into his arms.

Even damp with sweat she was delicious to hold. He should have let go, but she stared at him, stunned, and he felt afraid.

"What's wrong?" Emptiness filled her eyes.

"Nothing." She put her hands on his shoulders. Her fingers clung so hard, she almost pinched him.

"Beth, tell me. Is it Eli?" He didn't mean to shake her, but at least she seemed to move after. Then he realized she'd slid her arms around him. "You're hurt?" he asked, dreading the answer.

"Something's wrong with my son. Brent called with the results, and there's no physical reason for his problems. He… It's me—the divorce—not being able to rebuild the lodge right away."

"No, Beth." He stroked her hair. Her face fit into the hollow of his throat. Her breath on his skin made him shudder, but this was not about sex. It was about caring for her. "You can't blame Eli's problems on anyone or anything. Who knows what made him depressed?"

"I have to find out before something horrible happens to him, and he's not going to want to help himself."

"He's your son," he said, kissing her temple because he needed the feel of her skin against his lips. "You shouldn't be surprised he doesn't want help."

"I'd beg for help for him."

The tears in her eyes belied the defiant tilt of her chin, the touch-me-not tension in her back.

"I'll help you."

That was like waving a red flag in front of her face. She tried to pull away, but he let her go only as far as his hand on her arm.

"I'm not just talking because you're upset," he said. "Wise or crazy, inconvenient or not, I won't walk away."

"I can't believe you."

"I know."

"I want to." Longing, sweet and clear in her eyes, spoke when she couldn't, but he was strong enough to reach across her fear.

"Beth." He drew her arms around him. He was already kissing her when she linked her fingers behind him. The pressure of her palms in the small of his back cut his breath short.

Wrong time. Wrong place. Definitely the wrong woman, considering she lived an hour and a half from him with a troubled son who made him desperate to work a miracle.

But kissing Beth felt right. So right he had to pull her closer. He slid his hands into her hair, hungry for more. She tasted good. She opened her mouth. She might need no one, but she wanted him, and he had to prove he wasn't a man who left.

It wasn't so much a kiss as a lesson in survival. He'd met the threat of death. He wasn't sure he knew how to be even a figure of a father. But Beth made him forget everything except the most basic, desperate longing to be in her life.

She broke away first, breathing harshly. His heart was trying to explode again, but in an entirely different, pleasurable way.

"Is wanting me so wrong?" he asked.

"Eli comes first."

"You think I can't be good for him?" He held her hands in his, still at his back. "My father was always busy. I went alone to basketball games and Boy Scouts. Dad bought me a machine to pitch balls so I could learn to hit. He hired a tutor when I fell behind in history."

"Exactly what I don't want for Eli."

At forty-two, he'd turned down offers and temptations, knowing better than to mix his life with anyone who needed time. Why did Beth and Eli give him glimpses of a different choice? "I believe I know how to be a father because I wanted one when I was Eli's age."

"I must be out of my mind." Beth wiped her mouth.

"Getting rid of me won't be as easy as wiping away a kiss."

"My son needs me. You need to think about your health and your business. For all I know, you're helping us to appease your own guilt about your wife."

It was like being hit by one of those machine-pitched baseballs. She ran past him, and he let her go.

He wanted her more than he wanted to go back to work. And far from Eli's demands putting him off, he worried about the kid, too.

But *was* he jumping at a second chance to save someone? Could helping Eli make up for losing Madeline?

Didn't Beth deserve more?

"ELI?"

He froze and his starship got blasted all to hell. In his room, surrounded by pillows and a couple of manga, he'd been playing a game on the laptop. Comfortable for once in Uncle Van's house.

"Damn," he muttered.

"Eli? Are you here?"

His mother's fear both pleased him and worried him. He was tired of talking and mad at her for wanting to know every thought in his head, but did she have to act so scared all the time?

"What?"

"Oh." She sounded like he felt when his math

teacher called off a test. "There you are. Can we talk a minute?"

"Damn." He hit Pause on the game. "Here I come."

Waiting at the bottom of the stairs, she looked different, prettier. Her eyes were softer.

"What happened?" he asked.

"Nothing."

His mom was tough. She never acted like a girl, hardly wore makeup, and he wouldn't be surprised if she rebuilt the lodge board by board with her bare hands.

With her face red, she tried not to look at him. Then she did look, but turned away as if she couldn't stand him seeing her.

"Mom?"

"I got the loan today."

"Wow." He ran down the rest of the stairs and almost hugged her. Just in time to stop himself, he caught the banister and swung off it. "I'm glad." Now that all the old house was gone, maybe he wouldn't hate going there. It wouldn't look a fire pit.

"After they put the new foundation in, we'll have the walls framed, and then the drywall goes on. After that, I'll need help. You're a heck of a painter."

"Yeah. Okay." Painting might make up for what he'd done. He looked at a spot above her head. "When do you want me to start?"

"Mr. Grove is going to pour the foundation tomorrow if the weather holds, and then we'll start framing. Once the drywall is up, we can paint until we finish."

"I might be back at school."

"True, but wouldn't it be great if we were back in the house by summer?"

Her face looked funny again. "What else happened?"

She looked too hard into his eyes. "Brent called."

Just like that, he felt all sweaty. "Do I have to go back?"

"Not to him." She changed again—looked like when she found out Dirk Taft was stealing his lunch money. She didn't need armor like the guys in his video game. Swords would break when they hit her. "But he wants you to talk to some other people, and when we find someone you like, you can talk to her—or him—until you feel better."

"Don't act like I'm a little kid."

"Sorry. I don't know how to act about this."

"I don't want to talk to anyone." And tell he'd burned down their house? Nope.

"I'm sorry. I want to be your friend and keep you happy, but in this case, I have to be your mother and annoy you. You have to talk to one of these people— or someone else if you don't connect with anyone on this list."

And he was supposed to be happy? "You never make me do stuff I hate." That wasn't true. There was asparagus and a shower *every* night and "We can't afford a new skateboard."

"I have to this time."

To keep from crying like a baby, he dug his fists into his eyes. As soon as he couldn't see, his mother tried to hug him. He backed away. "Stop it."

"Eli, this is for your own good."

"You always say that. It's a great excuse. You start thinking something about me and I have to go to the doctor."

"Yes," she said, in a voice he didn't know. "You do have to go, but maybe after you talk, they'll say nothing's wrong."

He put his fists back in his eyes. He felt a weight—like one of those cartoon guys who sensed a big piano was hanging over his head. Even he doubted one of Dr. Brent's friends would say nothing was wrong.

"SO WHAT ARE YOU going to do next?" Van asked over the phone that night.

She balanced her elbow on the arm of his living room sofa. "I called and made appointments with all of them. We see one tomorrow, one the next day and the last one next Monday after Eli gets out of school."

"Will it work if Eli doesn't want to go?"

"I can't lurk around the house, listening at his door, hoping he starts to feel better."

He didn't say anything. She knew what he was thinking. Dragging Eli to a doctor wouldn't do him any good unless he took part in getting well.

"Did Brent have an idea what might be behind all this?"

"No more than I do. The obvious things are plenty. He hasn't enjoyed going to school here and that takes up most of his time. If he had more than a month left, I'd take him back to the old one."

"That wouldn't have worked for either of you in morning traffic."

"I should have rented a house closer to the lodge."

"Are you kidding? Waste money when you're trying to find more?" Van, calm and full of confidence, was just the prescription for her tonight. "Life keeps throwing obstacles at you, and you keep slugging away. Maybe this is when Eli learns to do that, too. Hey, wasn't your appointment with Jonathan Barr today?"

"I took the loan." She gave him the figures. "It won't be enough. I'm suddenly downsizing, but I guess I can build on later. They're pouring the foundation tomorrow unless it rains."

"Maybe we could talk about going into business together and adding cottages. You're land rich."

"Van." She almost asked him why he wouldn't tell her the truth about his own troubles. She stopped herself because she didn't like when he harassed her for the truth.

"I won't give up on this idea," he said. "I had plenty of time to think on the flight, and this would be a good investment."

"Are you serious?" An investment wasn't the same as a handout. "Could you afford it?"

"I'm serious, and I could find the money. The only problem I see is that we both like to take charge. Are you any good at compromise?"

"Not according to Campbell or Eli, and I know you're not."

"We'll talk about it when I get home. Have you checked on Aidan?"

Her throat tightened and her heart plummeted as she felt herself in his arms again. His kisses made her forget everything that mattered. She wanted only one more second of the closeness of his body against hers, his mouth drawing life from her, giving it back.

Thank God Eli couldn't be swept from her mind for long.

"I see him."

"You sound funny."

She scrambled for an excuse. "Because you keep accusing me of trying to kill him. He's fine. He also wanted to know about Eli, and I told him. He doesn't need anything for the house."

"Okay. Thanks."

"Sure."

"Someone's knocking at my door. I don't know if it's dinner showing up late, or my seven o'clock meeting."

"You'd better go."

"Let me know how Eli likes the doctors."

"Okay."

"And try to keep Mrs. Carleton from quitting."

"I try harder than you do. At least Eli and I pick up after ourselves."

"Because of guilt."

They hung up, laughing. She called Campbell to tell him what she was planning for their son. What a lucky night. She got his answering machine.

According to Eli, his father had avoided her calls before, but that was okay with her. If he'd acted like nothing was wrong with Eli, she'd have lost her temper, and he'd never appreciated her swearing-like-a-stevedore side.

She left the information and then dropped the phone on the cherry end table before flopping her legs over the end of the couch.

Then she heard the car. Starting and stopping. Despite dread almost gluing her to the chair, she ran for the garage.

It was cold. And dark, except for the light in her car illuminating Eli, who had eyes only for the dashboard in front of him. Good God, surely he wasn't trying to…

Beth hit the garage door opener. "Come out of there." Her own voice scared her. Harsh, a stranger's, thick with terror and furious.

Eli stared at her through the open driver's window. As a little boy, he'd taken her keys or Campbell's to "play drive" in the car. How many times had she and Campbell argued over the front seat of a car being an unsafe playhouse? Campbell had thought they should just hide their keys.

Find some calm. Don't make this worse.

She gulped one breath after another of the musty air. Crossing that painted, pale gray floor she felt as if she were watching herself march to the car.

She opened the door and then yanked Eli out. His shoulders felt fragile as balsa wood. She wanted to shake him and hug him so close he could never leave, and no one could get in to hurt him. And she needed to do it all at the same time. His dull eyes refused to focus on her.

"What are you doing?" she asked.

"Thinking."

"You don't think in a car with the engine on and the garage door shut."

He brought his hands up between them and shoved her away so that she staggered. "Let me go." He might have been sleepwalking.

She wanted to grab him again. Instead, she wrapped her arms around her own waist. If only someone could show her the right thing to do. "You could have killed yourself. Do I have to follow you around until we see that doctor in the morning?"

Her accusation finally shattered the fog. She knew the second he recognized her, but the boy inside his eyes was a stranger. Her blood froze.

"I'll go," he said.

"Go where?" Was he threatening her in that terrifying monotone? He wanted to run away?

"I need to feel normal, Mom. Nothing's happened, but I feel sad and bad. I'm always sad and I'm usually angry, and I always feel a little afraid, deep down, like something bad's about to happen. I'll go to that doctor if he can make it stop."

"Damn right you will." At his sullen look, she shut her mouth. She was the adult. Twisting fear into anger would only alienate him. "I'm sorry," she said. "You scared me, Eli. Why were you turning on the car with the door shut?"

He looked her straight in the eye. This time she saw her son starting to form inside those blank eyes. "I've done that a million times, Mom. You know I have."

"You've turned it on with the garage door open. You've never worked up a cloud of carbon monoxide."

"I never thought about the door being closed. If I had, I would have opened it. Mom, look at me. I'm not like other kids. Maybe you were never like me and you can't understand."

"You're eleven years old. You know better. I want to take you to the emergency room."

"No. I already agreed to go to that doctor tomorrow."

"And you were doing something that could kill you, son. You're too responsible to risk sitting in a running car in a closed garage, but if you were trying to—hurt yourself, you'd pretend this was nothing, just play—like when you were a kid."

"You're going to tell the doctor tomorrow. I'll

tell him. Would I do that if I was suicidal and trying to hide it?"

She looked at her son working so hard to make her believe. "You're not a child at all anymore."

"That's what I'm trying to tell you. So don't always be touching me. Don't try to make me feel better. I'm not sure anyone can."

She shivered. The sun never reached inside this building. The longer she stood here, the more it felt as cold as death. "Will you talk to Brent if I can get him on the phone?"

"No, Mom." He walked away. Taking the opportunity to dash tears out of her eyes, she didn't back down.

"Otherwise, we go to the hospital. I want to believe you, but I won't let you—"

"Die? You can see I don't want to do that. It's the last thing I—" He stopped, staring at her face as if he couldn't stand to see her.

No doubt she wasn't hiding anything. "I'll call Brent."

"All right." With his fists clenched, he stomped toward the house. Suddenly, he stopped and went back to open the back seat of the car.

Only then, did Beth see Lucy, nothing but a pair of eyes against the black upholstery. She tumbled to the floor, her nails scratching the surface. Then she grabbed at Eli's hand with her mouth. He brushed her away, but then patted her side.

Beth breathed again. He'd never hurt Lucy. No

matter what, Eli would protect his dog with his last breath. Just the way a mom would.

Lucy peered, her soulful brown gaze asking, "What next?" Beth rubbed her shoulder. She longed to pretend nothing could happen, but it was too late. "Let's go in and get Dr. Brent before he leaves his office."

"Can we wait until after Mrs. Carleton leaves? She was mean at lunchtime, like she thought I let you sleep on the couch to be funny. She asked me why I didn't wake you so you could sleep in your bed like decent folk."

"That sounds like Mrs. Carleton, but I'm sorry. We need to catch Brent tonight." He turned away. More mutiny. Fortunately they had a distraction who actually needed addressing. "Maybe you could give Mrs. Carleton a break? I don't know much about her, which is unusual around here, but she moved to Honesty when she was older. She may never have had children."

"Or she may have scared them so much they don't come see her."

"I meant she's not used to our noise or the way you and I are always running here and there. Van is more easygoing."

"And he's not here much, getting her house junky," Eli said.

"Mrs. Carleton has ideas about propriety. We'll move home as soon as we can, Eli. Learning to be patient with her might be good for both of us."

"Maybe you need a makeover. I don't." Sarcasm dripped from every word, but Beth smiled benignly, grateful for any emotion after a glimpse of that boy in the garage.

In the kitchen, she reached for the portable phone. Just after Eli was born, she'd memorized Brent's number without even meaning to.

"Can I talk to him privately for a minute?" she asked her son.

Eli left the room on a jet trail of resentment. Beth held out her hand as if she could drag him back.

This time Brent's receptionist put her through instantly. He picked up the phone and said a worry-tainted hello. "Something wrong?" he asked.

"I'm not sure." She explained what had happened. "He looked as if he were in shock, and he said he just wants to feel normal, but I seem to make it worse."

"Because you force him to pay attention to what's happening. Don't you, somewhere deep inside, wish you could put your head in the sand and pretend this will go away on its own?"

"Absolutely, and it's a relief to say so out loud."

"Did you think he was trying to kill himself, Beth?"

"No." She gripped the phone tighter. "He had Lucy in the back seat. He'd never harm her."

Brent tapped the phone with something. "Okay, but I have to ask. Are you sure he wouldn't think Lucy'd be better off if he sort of took her with him?"

"You don't have to pussyfoot around. I know what you mean and I'm positive. I see what kind of father he'll be in the way he cares for Lucy. He's not capable of hurting her."

"You'd bet his life on that?"

"Nearly. If you speak to him and feel satisfied that we can wait until tomorrow, I'll be his shadow tonight."

"Better let me talk to him. Remember though, I'm not a psychologist."

"But you've known him all his life."

She passed through every nook and corner on the way to Van's study where Eli had turned on the TV. Mrs. Carleton was nowhere to be found.

"Here you go." She handed him the phone. "Talk to him honestly if you can, Eli." He snapped his mouth shut and sat up, on the verge of telling her off.

She exited, trying to give him space to breathe.

CHAPTER EIGHT

THE FIRST NAME on Brent's list, a man who ordered them to call him Dr. Drayton, was a dismal failure. His office was all heavy slabs of furniture. His eyes held no compassion, though he boomed like a favorite old uncle when he spoke.

He left cigar stubs all over the place. A manly man, and too much so for her. But what about Eli? She had to let him decide.

"I'm just a blunt guy." Dr. Drayton showed them to straight-backed, cushionless chairs on the other side of his desk. "I'll always tell you what I think, and I'll suggest anything that makes Eli's life better, but Mrs. Tully, you may not hear what you want."

Beth concentrated on hiding her misgivings.

"How are the boy's grades?" Even though Eli was at her side, the doctor interrogated Beth, Marine style. Grades, friends, curfew, diet...

She cut in after he asked about pets. "Why don't you ask my son directly?"

"I'll talk to Eli in a moment."

He went on to sleeping habits, recent illnesses,

the number of hours Eli spent on the phone, on video games and online.

Beside her, Eli stewed in anger, and Beth didn't dare offer a hand to comfort him. Dr. Drayton wouldn't approve of the soft touch and Eli might bite her head off.

At last Dr. Drill Sergeant suggested she wait outside while he and Eli spoke. She went, cursing herself for letting him think he intimidated her, but this situation demanded restraint. A trait she'd never before practiced when anyone tried to interfere with her son.

Within a few minutes, Eli came out, too, red-eyed, stern, refusing to speak at all. Dr. Drayton asked Beth to come back. She hated leaving Eli.

"Mrs. Tully, your boy will be fine. Please join me."

She sat in the chair she'd vacated, whacking her spine against the no-frills wooden back.

"You're smothering your son," the man said.

She clutched the wooden seat. It was that or beat him about the head with the bronze eagle grounded on his desk. "Did Eli say I smother him?"

"You answered every question I asked you correctly. Should any mother know that much about her child?"

"If she's been worried about him, if she's involved with his school and if she lives in the same house with him. How would I not know about his friends?" Dear God, don't let me be driving my son to suicide.

"Don't get me wrong. I think we made progress," he said. "Eli's not used to a man's input, but we understood each other. He's reluctant to talk, but that's always true at a first visit when a little guy's mother is forcing him to see someone."

"You're implying I shouldn't insist?"

"No. No. But Eli's growing into a man. He needs a little less woman time. Seeing me will be good for him."

There it was. Another accusation of coddling. Could he be right? Was Eli simply trying to outgrow her?

"I can't pretend this isn't happening. I have to make sure he's all right."

"No, Mrs. Tully. You have to give him room. And I'm the man who can teach him to put a safe distance between you."

She sat back. "I'm everything bad in his life?"

"No." He laughed at her. Laughed. As if he were a sadistic clown, rather than a man charged with caring for emotionally troubled patients. She wanted to erase that smile from his he-man face. But she also needed to fall on her knees and beg for answers, in case he was right and she'd caused this trauma.

She rubbed her forehead and behind closed eyes, saw Eli again, stomping out to a chair in the waiting room.

"You're blind. You don't even see he's resentful and resistant," she said. "Not grateful you're riding in to save the day." Pressing her fingers to her lips, she tried to stop.

"You'll keep seeing me with your son. I can teach you both strategies—"

"I don't know how you keep your job, and you certainly won't be condescending to me or teaching my son to be a misogynist. As if he needs more problems."

Standing, she slid her purse between her elbow and side and sailed out of his office. Eli didn't look at her. She eased the doctor's door shut.

"I think we both need ice cream."

They went to their favorite specialty store. The drill sergeant would have assigned her extra duty, cleaning a toilet or something, which only made the ice cream taste sweeter. Eli managed to unlock his jaws enough to choke down a mixed slab of dairy cream and bubble gum with sprinkles on top.

When they got home, Beth parked in the garage and grabbed Eli's arm before he could get out of the car. "Want to go for a run?"

"Can Lucy come?"

"Sure."

"Do I have to go back to that guy?"

"Are you kidding me? I'm going to redo my will tonight with strict instructions that you're never to darken his door again." She took a deep breath. "Just in case."

Eli laughed. Red rimmed his eyes again. "I never thought I'd say this, but tonight I'm glad you make a big deal about the small stuff."

They left the garage and walked out the front to take the sidewalk to the porch. Morning sunlight had disappeared behind black and blue clouds, and rain began to slap the cement in fat drops.

"There goes our basement," Eli said.

If getting them back into their home didn't seem like a vital part of Eli's cure, she wouldn't have had the energy to care. The rain wetting their faces felt all too appropriate.

AFTER THEIR MEETING with the good Dr. Devastation, Beth found little jobs for Eli to do all day. That night, once he was in bed, she couldn't stop herself from strolling past his room. Again and again and then one more time.

Finally, she leaned her forehead against the door, praying he wouldn't open it to find her worrying so much she had to wait, listening for him to move. How many times had she leaned over his crib when he was a newborn, taking comfort from the slight elevation of his chest?

Eleven years later, watching made her sick.

At last she sat against the wall opposite his room and let the tears fall. She couldn't help it. She hadn't given in where Eli could see her. But during the dark hours of night-into-morning she fell apart.

At last, the sudden familiar grunt he'd always made as he turned—more like whirled—in his bed made it through the door. Beth pushed herself up the wall, wiping her face.

He hadn't refused to see the next doctor, and he was sleeping. She couldn't ask for more.

A home and a father at least as mature as his own son? She wouldn't let herself think of Aidan and the promises he'd nearly made.

For anything that extravagant, she'd still need a fairy godmother.

She stared at the telephone in her bedroom, but didn't touch it.

THE NEXT MORNING Beth woke reluctantly. She and Eli hardly spoke through breakfast. Moving her mouth cost too much energy, and the queasy feeling in the pit of her stomach refused to be ignored.

"I wish you'd calm down, Mom."

She concentrated on relaxing every muscle from her scalp down. "I'm making a mental list. We have so many things to do today, and I'm still hoping we get our basement."

"I'll bet the dirt doesn't dry out enough for Mr. Grove to go back."

"I called him last night. He said they'd almost finished putting the forms together."

"The forms to pour the cement in? Maybe tomorrow then."

"How do you know about that?"

"I hang around with the other guys. Their dads do stuff like that. Adam Grove was in my Geography class." He sounded wistful.

"If we ever have another accident like this, let's

rent a house in our old neighborhood." She pushed her spoon and napkin and bowl together, preparatory to getting up. "We'd better dress for your appointment."

"Here we go again."

"We'll find someone."

"I don't like the way people look at me."

"I don't blame you."

"I don't like the way you look at me."

Her queasiness welled. "I'm sorry. I'd love to be the stoic type, and I keep thinking I'm hiding what I feel, but I don't seem to be keeping you safe."

"Whatever."

He picked up his cereal bowl and set it in the sink with a rattle that made her get up and check for cracks after he walked out of the room.

"What's wrong?"

"Mrs. Carleton." Beth almost dropped the bowl as she faced the other woman. "Aren't you early today?"

"No."

She was, but talk about a pointless argument. Beth had no urge to mentally arm wrestle the formidable housekeeper. "Nice to see you. We're going out."

"I've heard."

"Huh?"

"The boy's in trouble. I've overheard folks talking in town."

A mother's protective rage electrified—damn near shorted Beth's brain. "Mrs. Carleton, I've tried to stay out of your way and make no extra work. I'm not sure why you don't like us or why you always hid your animosity until my brother invited us to stay, but I had better never hear you've said one word against Eli."

"Calm down, Mrs. Tully." The other woman set two net bags of shopping on the island and tried to cool Beth with one of her icy glances. "I was going to ask if I could do anything to help you or your son. You probably won't be surprised to hear I have a little depression myself. I thought the boy was upset, and if you need any extra help with him, babysitting, whatever, I'd be glad to help." She looked even colder when she was trying to be kind.

"I see—no, I don't."

"I don't dislike you two, but I get attached to people who stay awhile. I don't want to be attached." She opened the strings on the first bag and pulled out a sack of sugar. "And pardon me for being blunt, but you're not the tidiest guests who've ever visited Mr. Haddon."

Beth understood the part about not wanting to get attached. She found herself checking for Aidan's car at all hours. "I've misjudged you."

Mrs. Carleton looked disappointed. "I expected something a little sharper from you, Mrs. Tully."

"I wish you'd call me Beth."

"Feeling egalitarian now that I've confessed to having a soft heart?"

"I heard nothing about soft." Smiling felt odd, but

good. Mrs. Carleton might look like Lot's wife after she'd turned into salt, but she was trying to reach out. Abandoned by her own husband, she'd understand Beth's reasoning. "I hate hearing my last name." More than ever right now.

Mrs. Carleton stopped in the middle of putting eggs in the fridge. "Why didn't you change it back?"

"Because of Eli. I wanted us to have the same name."

"Ahhh. I never had that problem."

"Why didn't you take back your maiden name?"

"Women didn't do that when I got divorced." She shut the refrigerator with a shove that rattled every glass object. "Do you want breakfast?"

End of conversation. Beth shook her head. "We just finished. I'll do our dishes before—"

"Cleaning the kitchen is my job. I'm sure you have more pressing commitments."

"I can—"

Mrs. Carleton turned with a look, clearly preferring to be alone while her confessions still wavered in the kitchen air.

Beth lifted both hands. "I meant thanks." She hurried down the hall and up the stairs to her room to change and get ready for running the next stage of the therapist gauntlet.

She'd lived in Honesty almost all her life, but the people still surprised her. Imagine Mrs. Carleton guarding her tender center with intimidating crankiness left over from a bad divorce.

Beth didn't want to be that way.

She wanted to believe again. She wanted to believe Aidan when he swore he'd keep promises and went out of his way to care for her and Eli.

As Beth turned from her closet, pulling a T-shirt over her head, she caught sight of the cottage roof. What was he doing?

Had he thought of the kisses she'd walled off in a compartment that had no door? She'd dated since the divorce. She'd shared kisses.

None of them had touched her, tempted her, unnerved her the way his had. Muttering with frustration, she grabbed a pair of jeans and shimmied into them. Her son's reaction to Aidan's certain departure didn't bear considering if she wanted to keep her grip on sanity.

"Mom?" He thudded on her door with surprising force.

"Coming." She twisted her hair into a ponytail and stepped into flip-flops as she crossed to open up for him. "Ready?"

"I've been waiting for you." He looked at the watch his father had given him two years ago. The woven band had begun to fray, but Eli refused a replacement. He kept saying he'd ask his dad for a new one.

Bitterness choked Beth. Eli probably had asked, but Campbell had most likely turned him down.

"Let's go." She shut her door with a shudder at her unmade bed. "And pray Mrs. Carleton doesn't set foot in there."

"She's all over this place." He led the way downstairs. "Mom, don't I seem okay?"

"Not all the time."

"I'm fine, though. Why do I have to go to another doctor?"

"Maybe you feel all right now because you know you're going to get help." She'd read that online. "What if something went wrong? The house burned again? Or you got a grade you didn't like at school? What if something made you sad?"

"I'm not a baby. It's more than sad."

Why did Campbell get to be so oblivious, but Eli had to be self-aware and mature? "That's why you're going. You know it's worse than being normally sad."

"Okay, but I don't want anyone yelling at me."

"I'm going to ask Brent why he sent us to that lunatic. He actually said he would have taken his kid to any of these therapists. Brent must know him from conferences when he's on his best behavior."

"What if Dr. Brent was wrong about all the doctors he told you about?"

"We'll find someone else."

In the car, they were both too anxious to talk. Today's counselor, Dr. Kathy Lester, had her offices in the medical building. "Since Brent's in the same building with Dr. Lester, maybe he knows her better."

"Is that supposed to be good?" Eli asked.

"I hope." She turned past the courthouse and wove through back streets.

"I thought Aidan might come by last night."

"He's got that laptop and I guess his folks and the doctors have kept him from working until now. He's probably a workaholic." She had to prepare Eli for the day Aidan left.

"I've heard of workaholics on TV." He didn't say whether he thought it was a good thing or bad.

"I should have called him. He wants to know how you feel about the doctors."

"Does he?" Eli's smile broke her heart. She shouldn't have said anything.

"Here we are." She hit the blinker and turned into the parking lot.

"Let me get the ticket." He unlatched his seat belt, leaned across her and plucked the ticket from the machine at her open window.

"Seat belt back on."

"Do I take this in for validation?" He balanced the ticket on his forehead, but then sighed when Beth refused to move the car. "We're in the lot. I'm safe." Finally, he latched the belt again.

"She's on the twelfth floor. We can cross on the skywalk at the fifth."

"Okay, but we could go to the basement and then up."

"We could do that a couple of times and maybe Dr. Lester would close her office for the night before we arrive."

Worse than that, they ran into Aidan. She sensed Eli's excitement before she saw Aidan. She looked up and locked onto a pair of eyes that made her wish she and Eli could stay with him.

"How are you?" he asked Eli.

She looked at the cars passing beneath them, the sky above, the frail-looking metal frame that sheltered them between the medical complex buildings.

"We're going to see another doc. I'm sick of it," Eli said.

"How was yesterday's?"

"A nut," Beth said without thinking. "I mean he wasn't right for us."

"You're not seeing him again?"

"I think Mom was rude to him."

"I lost my temper, but I couldn't help it. How about you, Aidan? Are you all right?"

"I saw the cardiologist my doctor recommended, and he says I can resume normal activities."

Beth breathed easier, but tried not to show her relief. "You're going to be okay?" she asked, spoiling it.

He nodded, his eyes bemused.

"Are you leaving?" Eli asked, and he couldn't be more anxious than she to hear Aidan's answer.

"I'm not that free. I can run instead of walk and I have permission to start looking at my work. I can see what's going on with the company from the laptop I just bought, but Van and I already agreed I'd stay in the cottage for a month."

"A month?" It sounded like such a short time.

"Mom said you were a workaholic."

Beth blushed even though Aidan only laughed. His husky voice caressed her. If her son weren't in trouble and Aidan weren't so temporary, she could have nestled into the sound of his laughter.

"The heart attack taught me a lesson," Aidan said. "I want some life to go with my work. I keep telling your mom."

He shouldn't say things like that in front of her son. She set her hand against Eli's back. "We'll be late."

"If you want to play a game, Aidan," Eli said, "I'll bring one down tonight."

"We're going to the lodge." Beth grabbed at the first excuse. "You won't be home in time to play."

Aidan was a little smoother. "Sorry about that," he said. "We'll have to work something out for when your mom can spare you."

"Aww," Eli said, "I never have anyone to play with at Uncle Van's."

"All the more reason to get your house built, huh?" Aidan chucked Eli's forearm. "Maybe I'll drop by to see the progress."

"Good," Eli said. "See you around, Aidan."

"Okay. Bye."

"Bye."

Aidan passed them, leaving a whiff of soap and sunshine that was fast becoming Beth's favorite scent. She tore her gaze away from his back and bumped into Eli's indignant stare. For a second, she felt as if she were the child.

"Did you tell Aidan to stay away from us? Why are you making sure he won't hang around?"

They'd have plenty to discuss with this Dr. Lester. Like how to hide being shifty when she was trying to save her son from disappointment and loneliness.

"I didn't say anything to Aidan." She glanced at her watch—it wasn't there, but she acted as if she'd seen a fast-moving clock. "We're going to be so late."

"I'm mad at you, Mom."

"At least you don't have a hard time saying so." She hurried him the rest of the way across the skywalk and into the nearest elevator, prepared to confess everything to Dr. Lester after the woman talked to Eli.

They didn't have to wait long outside the office. They'd barely sat in plush blue chairs when they were called.

A young woman who didn't look at Eli funny showed them back to a bright, airy office, bounded on one wall by windows. Another woman stood and came around her desk. She led the way to a seating arrangement of two squat sofas, and she sat beside Eli.

"I'm Dr. Lester."

"I'm Eli. You don't have to be all nice."

"It's habit." She picked up a pillow from behind her back and fluffed it, as if she were at home. "How are you?" she asked.

"I don't know why I have to be here."

She touched the folder on her coffee table. "Brent gave me some notes so I'd know a little bit about you." She glanced at Beth. "You've known Brent since you were both children?"

Beth nodded, her faith a little dented after yesterday. "He explained the problems Eli's having?"

"Yes, but I'd like to hear what Eli thinks. Brent may not know what Eli considers most important."

Beth sat back in her chair, trying not to burst into the "Hallelujah Chorus." Dr. Lester was treating Eli as a mature boy, not a mollycoddled baby. They might just stand a chance.

Eli appeared to disagree. He shut down as if he didn't care about feeling anything at all, much less normal. Getting information from him was like pulling one of those monster trucks he liked so much.

"If you had to guess, Eli, why would you say you were here?"

"I'm sad," he said, "and lately, I'm angry a lot, but my mom's making me see doctors all over the place." He looked a little shamefaced. Obviously, Beth wouldn't have forgotten their conversation about seeing anyone who could make him feel better.

"Do you think you might be overreacting, Mrs. Tully?"

"No, but I don't mind if Eli does as long as we're getting him help."

"You don't mind being wrong?"

Why would that matter? "I just want my son to be all right."

"Good." She chatted with Eli some more, about school and his old friends, his new friends and his impatience with living with Van. "I think we have a nice start." Her serenity eased the stiffness in Beth's spine. "Try to stop feeling anxious, both of you. We'll work together, and everything will be all right again."

Eli looked back at her, silent. Beth wished he'd say something. He didn't. Dr. Lester nodded.

"Eli, may I have a moment with your mother?"

Eli trudged out of the room, closing the door.

"I'm never sure what he's thinking these days," Beth said, "but I'd like to tell you what he did the night before last." Knowing they weren't going to see him anymore, she hadn't mentioned the garage episode to Dr. Drayton, but she described it to Dr. Lester.

"You don't think he was trying to find the courage to harm himself?"

"No, because of our dog. He loves her too much to hurt her. I wish he loved himself as much."

"You still need to keep a good eye on him. I'd like to have another word with him before you go."

Beth nodded. "Do you think you'll be able to help if he won't talk?"

"This was our first meeting. He may be reluctant to talk with you in the room. Boys his age are often unwilling to share their deepest feelings with their mothers." Dr. Lester opened the folder and ran her finger down the first page. "Brent tells me your ex-husband is not overly involved with Eli?"

Beth hardly knew how to answer.

The doctor studied her notes again. "I understand, but maybe we could persuade him to visit just once, so I can see how they respond to each other."

Beth picked up her purse. "I'll try, but I'm sorry I can't promise to get him here without a cop and some handcuffs."

"It happens that way. Does Eli realize his father is—"

"I'm not sure what Eli thinks about Campbell. He hasn't asked me much about his dad."

Dr. Lester stood and Beth followed. "Mrs. Tully, your son probably knows more than he's saying."

"I guess I've been trying not to notice."

"Human nature, but you should also stop worrying." She walked with Beth toward the door. "It affects Eli. You're doing the right thing for your son, and it won't harm anyone if we all talk together for the first few visits. I'll see Eli first and then I'll ask you in. You talk to him and if he's amenable, call back and make an appointment."

"I feel lucky we've found you, though Eli does have the final say. I imagine Brent told you he gave us a list of several names. We still have one more appointment next Monday, and then I'll get back to you with Eli's decision."

"Sounds good. If you call, make an appointment with my receptionist and we'll get started."

Dr. Lester leaned around the door. "Can I see you a second more, Eli?"

He strolled past Beth, intent on remaining untouchable. The doctor closed her door.

Beth sat in one of the blue chairs. She took out her phone and checked for messages. There were none. She stared at her watch. The office door remained closed. She went to the window and counted the cars in the lot below. Fifteen and a Vespa.

The door finally opened again. Dr. Lester held it with her hand above Eli's head as he came out. "Nice meeting you."

He nodded, but his face was a thundercloud. "Nice to meet you, too."

Dr. Lester lifted a beckoning hand to a man in the corner of her waiting room. Beth collected Eli and they left the office. Beth closed the door before she spoke.

"Wasn't she perfect?"

"Perfect?" He rolled his eyes so hard it was a wonder they didn't fly right out of his head. "No, Mom, she wasn't perfect. She was you."

CHAPTER NINE

THEY DROVE from the medical center to the lodge. For once, Beth was the one who needed physical work, and she needed it bad. She parked in her usual spot, down the hill from where her old front door used to stand.

"Coming up?" she asked Eli.

"I've got a headache, Mom. And a stomachache."

"And you don't want to talk to me about the doctor. I get it. In fact, I don't want to talk, either." She got out and shut the car door with more enthusiasm than strictly necessary. Immediately, hip-hop began to vibrate through the whole vehicle. It didn't seem to add to Eli's suffering.

Muttering about the unfairness of allowing one's adolescent son a say in his own therapist, Beth climbed the hill to the throng of men crowded around the open wound of her basement. Sam was in the gaping hole, hammering the last few nails into the last of the cement forms.

"Hey, Beth."

"Trey." She hugged the man who came out of

the crowd. "Good to see you. Thanks for coming back."

"I'm glad to help. Sam gave us a call, said if we were off duty again, we could save you some money if we built forms."

"I should have been here, too."

"No." He hitched his chin toward the rocking car. "Ann told me you had some appointments. How's that going?"

She'd just as soon Eli's business not travel through town. "How did she hear?"

"She heard you all saw Brent late one night and he referred you."

"Someone in his office needs to be fired." He looked affronted and she took it back. "I'm sorry. I don't want anyone thinking something's wrong with Eli."

"Especially not his friends. Don't worry."

"People keep saying that to me today."

"What are you two whispering about up there?" Sam asked. "You don't like the forms, Beth?"

"Are you kidding? I've rarely seen a more exquisite sight." She leaned in. "How are you going to pour the cement? The truck won't get this close, will it?"

"We have the equipment, madam, and if this sun stays with us, we'll have a basement by nightfall."

"And my gratitude for the rest of our lives."

"Hear that, guys?" He took a last whack with the hammer and lifted his hand. Jim grabbed it and Sam walked up the wall with his help. He dropped the hammer on a tarp and pulled his phone out of his pocket. "I'm going to check on the truck, but it should be here any second. You guys can go now," he said.

One by one, the other men said their goodbyes, waving at Eli as they walked past him. Trey nudged Beth as he started down the hill. "Why don't I take him with me? The other guys are skating again today."

Beth eyed her son. "I don't know. He said he was feeling punky."

"Who wouldn't be? Give him a break."

"If you're sure you don't mind. I'll call Ann to find out when I can pick him up."

"Why not let him stay the night?"

"Thanks, Trey." She squeezed his forearm. "But I don't need a break, and I'd worry about him. When the cops called you at 3:00 a.m., you'd look out your window and find me lurking in the yard."

Trey brushed away a bee, drawn to sweat and the new life of spring. "Think about it. Eli's always welcome with us, and we'd remind him he has friends."

"Maybe you're right. I guess he can go if he feels all right."

Trey went down the hill and knocked on the car window. Eli put it down. He listened to whatever Trey said and then leaned out.

"It's okay, Mom?"

"Sure, if you feel all right."

"I'm great." He shut the window and clambered out of the car. He got so excited he ran to catch up with his friend's father, but then U-turned back to slam the door shut.

"What's wrong with Eli?" Sam asked, putting his phone away.

"A stomachache, he said, but he seems better." They shared a wry grin. "Where's the truck?"

"Stuck at a red light at the courthouse. You don't have to wait. You can't help with this."

"I want to see, Sam. Finally, we're moving forward."

"Speaking of which, when are the framers set to come?"

"I haven't scheduled them, since we didn't know about the basement."

"Because the weather's been damp, set them up for the morning after tomorrow." All around them, the sky was dark, and the air so moist it curled Beth's hair. Sam dropped his arm across her shoulder. "Go home and try to schedule all your contractors. We'll finish quicker here if we don't have to worry about the home owner falling in."

"Funny, Sam."

"You won't be laughing when you find you can't get a framing crew for another month. Think how much building you've seen around town."

"And in the neighborhoods." She opened her purse and felt around for her keys. "What was I thinking?"

Halfway to the car, she remembered her keys

were in the ignition. Else, the hip-hop couldn't have been rocking her own neighborhood. "Oh, no."

She ran the last few yards, skidding down the hill to thud into the side of her car. Sure enough, the keys were dangling from the ignition, on a leather plait Eli had made for her in Cub Scouts. She yanked his door handle, grunting.

It didn't open. Her door. She ran around the old Ford.

Sadly, she'd fallen into the habit last fall of not locking her doors. She'd concentrated so much lately on locking them that she tended to hit the locks when she got out. She couldn't blame Eli for doing the same thing.

"Are your keys inside?" Sam asked. "I have a hammer."

She tried to laugh, pushing sweaty hair out of her eyes. "Can you believe this?"

"You're having a bad day?"

"A little disappointing, and I definitely can't afford a locksmith."

"Don't you have an extra key at Van's?"

"Thanks for reminding me." She grabbed her phone, lodged in her jeans pocket. Just above the number for Van's house was the number for Van's cottage.

Locking keys in a car was hardly tidy, and Mrs. Carleton wouldn't approve.

Nevertheless, she dialed the house. Mrs. Carleton answered on the first ring.

"This is Beth."

"So I saw on that caller ID thing."

"Mrs. Carleton, I've locked my keys in the car." No doubt the other woman was shaking her head with much despair. "I hate to put you out, but would you mind bringing me the spare?"

"I'd do it right away, but my car's in the shop. I came to work in a taxi."

"A taxi?" Thunder rumbled overhead. Beth peered up. No rain, please. No rain.

"Don't worry," Sam said. "It's only thunder. There's no rain in the forecast."

At the same time, Mrs. Carleton went on. "What if I call the cottage? That nice man down there might bring it."

"I don't think—"

"Nonsense. I'll give him this number and have him call you if he can come." She hung up, taking matters into her own hands.

Aidan called within seconds. Beth choked out his name, overly aware of Sam at her side.

"It's Beth," she said, flustered as if she'd just been kissed.

"I called you," he said.

"Oh, yeah. I have a huge favor to ask."

The cement mixer rumbled up the lane. Its driver shifted gears.

"I can't hear you, Aidan. Just a second," Beth said. The truck brushed honeysuckle, and the smell wafted by. The truck made a turn up the ragged driveway and eventually came to a halt. "Aidan? Are you still there?"

"Mrs. Carleton told me you'd locked your keys in. I'm just calling before I go pick up the spare. Are you both okay, other than not being able to get in the car? I heard thunder."

"We're fine, and the weatherman just told me we're not expecting rain." His concern felt so good she couldn't afford to get used to it.

"Where are you?"

"That's the imposition. I'm at the lodge."

"I've been going crazy, stuck in this house—however nice it is. You're giving me an excuse to get out."

"Thanks, Aidan." Beth closed her phone and put it back in her pocket and felt silly for being excited. Sam had already gone back up the hill. She climbed up, too.

The cement mixer roared. No one spoke as the forms filled. She let herself imagine the new lodge. It would be as austere as ever since she'd hadn't received the extra money to install a few luxuries, but she couldn't wait to open her doors again.

"That housekeeper of Van's is scary." Sam all but yelled in her ear.

"Terrifying, but I think she has a soft center."

"God forbid I should be around her long enough to stumble across it. I'm telling you my children turn the other way in the grocery store when we run into her."

"That's not nice, Sam." Unexpectedly, the

cement mixer shut down when she was in midsentence. Sam's assistant and the driver turned.

"What are you doing to Beth, Sam?"

She laughed and so did he. The men joined in until the cement mixer kicked back on.

Beth waved at Sam to get his attention. "Thanks for everything."

"I'll call you when we finish—let you know how things stand before I go home."

"Are you sure I shouldn't stay?"

"We're fine without your direction. You've seen where we're pouring. Everything else is gravity."

She leaned against her car, far enough away that she could only see the men from the waist up. Distance also buffered the noise.

Soon, a car turned into the lane between the budding Bradford pears. Aidan.

The last time they'd been together without Eli as an audience, she'd been in his arms.

He had no idea how she wanted to be with him again. To forget they came from different worlds, that his wanting to be with her and Eli might have more to do with guilt over his former wife. Needing him was more precious to her because she hadn't expected to feel so much for any man. It was like growing up instead of playing at the marriage she'd endured.

He parked behind her and got out, dangling the key from one finger. "Mrs. Carleton looked a bit put out. You should let her cool off."

"You're reading her wrong. She suggested

calling you." Beth took the key and put it in her door, as if it might not fit. Anything to hide the way he made her tremble.

The lock opened perfectly.

"Thanks," she said. "I'm grateful."

"I can imagine." He glanced toward the building site. "How's it going?"

"They're pouring the basement. In three months I'll be back in business."

"Three months? That's not long."

"It's not going to be a big house. A room for me and one for Eli, and four more for desperate fishermen."

"Only four? And why desperate?"

"I couldn't afford to build a larger house." She stared intently at the scarred hillside. "I was hoping to add extras, a hot tub in the back, more family friendly furniture in the rooms, frills here and there to make it cozy for wives and children."

"Why?" A businessman, he couldn't avoid being interested. He craned to see what went on above them. "You didn't have those things before, but the place worked for you?"

"I held my own, but we had men who came strictly for the fishing. I hoped to attract their families for vacations. A week's stay in lovely Virginia, however backwoods," she said, lifting her voice over a new load of cement, "pays me better than a long weekend with a bunch of smelly guys talking up their favorite bait."

"Why can't women be happy with us the way we are?"

"You take fishing breaks?"

"I haven't before." He nodded toward the men and the machines on the hill. "You won't invite me up to see?"

Not a chance. Every time she saw him, she craved more time with him. While he tried for a glimpse of her new basement, she gave in to temptation, checking out his jeans and white shirt and the hint of muscle underneath.

His smile, wide and somehow soft, made her feel vulnerable. "If you look at me like that, telling me to go away won't work."

Why pretend he was wrong? "Sorry. I should go. I have to schedule the framers and—"

"Have you eaten lunch? Come out with me."

"Are you kidding? Everyone who sees us will tell everyone they know, and then those people will tell their friends, and before you know it, they'll have you living here and I'll be getting the broadest hints that you're way out of my league. Worst of all, Eli will start assuming you'll be around."

"What the hell is that out of your league crap?"

She preened a little, sliding her hands over her hips. "It sounds nice the way you put it, but as much as I love living here, that's how people would see you and me together."

"You paint an attractive picture of small-town life."

"I know my own friends."

"Friends?"

"They'd mean well." She waved a hand toward Sam. "And I'm feeling the same about Eli. He likes hanging out with you. The male attention is good for him, but you're a visitor."

"I keep trying to tell you I like it here," he said, "except for the boredom factor of not being able to do the things I want to. That wouldn't always be a problem."

"I can't risk a relationship right now."

"Even I see this isn't the time to discuss it," he said, "but why do you assume the worst?"

Because it had taken her years to assume the worst about Campbell? She didn't intend to make another mindless decision about a good-looking man.

"I can't, Aidan. Please, let's talk about something else. Or better yet, get going."

He chose a change of subject. "Why can't you afford to add luxury to your lodge? I don't see that many guys going on vacation without their wives and children, and you might bring in more paying customers."

"We had a steady business, but it wasn't enough for the loan I wanted." Aidan was still recovering. And now, besides not wanting to kill him, she'd also prefer he didn't think she was angling for an investment. "I still think families are the way to go."

"But?"

"But it's not your problem."

"I'm curious." He took her hand. "Call it a personality quirk."

His fingers around hers suggested other ways to touch. She couldn't think.

"Beth?"

"My husband was supposed to pay the insurance premium—our house insurance—according to the divorce decree. The company that held the policy didn't tell me when he stopped paying, and we weren't covered when the house burned." She tugged gently, instinctively wanting to stand away from him, on her own.

"And Van wouldn't help?"

She went for the car door. "This talk is turning too personal. I have a son to care for and a house and a business to build, and your life is waiting for you in D.C."

"Let me talk to Van."

"No one needs to talk to Van."

"Then explain. He'd never let you go without. Especially when it comes to money. When he has all he'll need and then some. I don't see it."

"Leave it alone, Aidan. Now you're talking about my family."

His self-deprecating laugh stopped her from leaving. "Remember what we know about each other. I don't walk away from trouble, and you were born to nurture."

"I wasn't."

"You try to be tougher than you are, according to Eli."

"I'm rebuilding my home. That and the thought of my son being ill are all that matters to me now."

"I wish you were brave enough to take a chance on me. I'm good for more than delivering keys." He started toward his own car, and then looked over his shoulder. "You wouldn't want to tell me how Eli's visit went?"

He had a right. He'd found her son and made her see she had to act.

"I liked today's doctor. Eli didn't."

"Didn't?"

"I thought she was perfect. He thought she was like me." Despite her iron will and perfect independence, she felt like crying. That must have shown, too.

Laughing, Aidan came back. She didn't realize he was going to reach for her until he did.

"He's just a kid," Aidan said against her hair.

She tried to hold back, but he didn't seem to realize he shouldn't offer comfort. She leaned against him, just a little, not enough to commit. "I love that boy more than my own life, but he's killing me."

"He'll straighten things out with a therapist who can help him. And you can come talk to me if you won't speak with a counselor. I promise not to assume you want more than talk."

The truth lay between them, seductive and forbidden. Their need for each other was growing despite any fight she put up.

"Trust me a little, Beth."

"I'm trying."

His mouth tightened, and he let her go. Contrarily, she wished he hadn't.

"That ex-husband of yours has a lot to answer for. I'm even more pissed when I think of him leaving you and Eli high and dry. And I'm still surprised at Van."

"Don't be. You're right about Van. He begged me to let him help, but I'm allergic to charity, especially from someone who loves me. Eli needs to see me take out a loan and pay it back. We can work on our own house—even if he has been skating out."

"He ducks out of helping?" Aidan shoved his hands into his pockets and laughed at her affront. "Sorry, but he's usually so grown up he scares me."

"He's the best," she said, "but he's a kid. Hanging out with his friends is a lot more entertaining than helping me tear down a house. Aidan?"

He nodded.

"You have to leave him alone. He's getting attached to you."

Anger forced his eyes into slits. Then something made him look over her shoulder. "Maybe we should go. One of those guys has been watching us for a while, and I don't want people talking about you."

"Any chance he's admiring the pear trees? The

last thing we need to do is fire up the gossip machine."

"I'm not sure anyone up there is a pear-tree kind of guy." Aidan stared into the woods, turning his back on the semi-orchard in question. "Which ones are they?"

CHAPTER TEN

"PICK UP, PICK UP, pick up, Dad." Eli hit his desk so hard Lucy raised her head to stare at him with sad eyes. "Sorry," he said.

She dropped her head onto her paws.

At last, there was a click and his father said hello.

"Dad?"

"Eli, hey, son. How ya been?"

"Okay, okay. I've been trying to call you all day."

"I know. I had some—business. I would have called you back."

"I called you at your work, but they said you quit again."

"I had a better offer. You gotta go where the money is, man."

Yes. Talk about great news. His dad had more money now. "I'm glad." Eli tried not to jinx himself, sounding happy. "I have a favor to ask."

"What kind of favor?"

"I was at Jeff's yesterday."

"Again? Where was your mom?"

"Working on the house. Listen, Jeff's father is

going to help him make his own skateboard—a custom skateboard, and he said he'd help me, too, if I bought a kit."

"What does your mom say?"

"I didn't ask her. I know she doesn't have the money, but maybe you could help me."

"Well, you know, I'm just starting this new gig."

"New what?"

"Job. And money is short."

"You said you'll make more."

"I won't get paid for a few weeks, maybe longer. And you know how much I have to give your mom. I'm strapped."

"When I start getting allowance again, I'll pay you back, but I have to get the kit now, and I don't have enough saved. I need about forty dollars."

"How much have you saved, son?"

"Seventy. Mom made me put it in the bank so I was lucky. It didn't get burned up."

"That was smart. Sounds like you could lend me some dough, buddy."

"Huh?"

"Just kidding. Kidding, but you talk to your mom about this skateboard thing. Isn't that why I give her money?"

"I should've known you'd make up reasons not to help me. And you're crazy if you think I don't know you don't want to give Mom anything." He hung up, gasping like a fish jerked out of the lake, half expecting his father to call right back and yell at him.

He didn't.

Eli dropped onto his back on the bed and pulled the comforter completely around himself. In the dark, he didn't care if he cried. His mom couldn't get scared. His dad couldn't tell him to be a man.

The dark felt good, cool and empty. It made him feel safe. No one could see him. He couldn't even see himself.

He climbed off the bed, pulling the comforter with him and covered Lucy with it, too. She struggled, but he wrapped an arm around her neck and she stayed.

"Thanks, girl." He laid his head against her belly, and her breathing made him feel better, but he made sure no light could get to her or him.

"Why, Lucy?" he asked. "Jeff's father's not rich, but he helped Jeff buy his. Why won't my dad?" Lucy grunted. "Maybe Mom?"

He couldn't even ask. He'd burned down the house. She wouldn't take the money he'd saved, but he'd bet she wouldn't let him spend it, either.

"Eli?"

Her voice came from downstairs. He rolled out of the blanket and threw it toward the bed. Then he stared at the window. This house didn't have a roof that sloped all the way to the ground. He couldn't jump down and escape.

But there was his closet.

Hurrying, he tripped over a corner of the comforter and almost fell. Lucy grunted, but she didn't raise her head this time. He opened the closet door and jumped inside.

Darkness wrapped him up again.

"ELI?" Beth tapped on his door and then opened it. Lucy looked up from the floor. "Where's Eli, girl?"

Lucy only stared. Beth walked inside and looked behind the door. She found a pair of shoes and Eli's jacket, which he hadn't worn in days. No boy, though. Butterflies danced in her belly.

The desk chair was pulled away from the desk. The comforter lay half on the floor, which was odd because he'd been good about making his bed before Mrs. Carleton could get to it.

"No need to panic, huh, Lucy?"

Lucy still stared.

Beth remade the bed. She'd only called him to make sure he was out of the way while she used the phone. "I'll look for him after I talk to Campbell."

She went downstairs and opened the front door. Mrs. Carleton walked behind her with a dusting cloth.

"Have you seen Eli?" Beth asked.

"Not for a while. You chase after that boy too much."

"So I keep hearing."

"Let him alone and he'll show up. Any boy likes to go out to the woods. Where's the dog?"

"In his room." She'd love to believe he was roaming the woods. Just the other night, it had been chilly, still more winter than spring, but a few days' sunlight and warmth had changed the world. The trees were beginning to clothe themselves in leaves. The air here and at the lodge smelled of honeysuckle.

"She's in his room, but he's not?" Mrs. Carleton dusted a table stridently. "That's different, but he has worried about taking her outside since the accident."

"I'll look for him in a few minutes. I have to make a phone call."

The other woman went about her business. Beth went into Van's office to get the phone from his desk. Dialing Campbell's number, she went outside, onto the porch. He finally picked up as she turned the corner on the verandah to the back of the house.

"Eli, I told you, I can't—"

"You called him? Campbell, I'm so glad. Did you make plans already?" For once, she hadn't needed to remind him this was his weekend.

"Beth."

In the time he took to say her name, she recovered her grasp of reality. "Did you tell him you couldn't pick him up again?"

"Not yet, but you tell him for me. I hate to disappoint him."

"You hate to? But it's okay for me to do your dirty work? What did you talk to him about?"

"Do you have to know every word that passes between me and my son?"

"Right now, yes. No matter what you think, something is wrong with him, and you're not helping."

"He just called me, and he sounded fine. Give the guy a break."

"Thanks, Campbell. Great advice, as always."

"I don't have to take this."

"You do have to help take care of your son. Why don't you want to see him?"

"I told him already, but I'm about to start a new job."

"A new job?" That fish story had lost its luster years ago. "You quit again."

"Quit? I'm moving on to something better."

Story of his life, and pointless to call him on it. "You're working this weekend?" What a joke. He'd never take a job that interfered with his precious weekends. Too many parties to attend—where he mooched off the friends he'd managed to keep.

"You always assume the worst."

She went farther around the porch, not wanting even Mrs. Carleton to hear. Her shoes thudded as if she'd suddenly gained fifteen pounds. The weight of anger.

"You quit another job because they were garnishing your wages for child support. How is paying to help keep Eli in clothing and food some kind of an option for you? Why don't you want to keep him safe and put a roof over his head?"

"I'm not perfect like you."

"If I were perfect, I'd never have fallen for your game." She took a deep breath. "This gets us nowhere, and I have to find Eli. You won't be paying child support this month and you won't be picking him up this weekend?"

"I told you, I can't."

"You'd better be careful. Your son is feeling doubt about everything in his life. What will you do if he stops believing you love him? How long do you think I can cover for you?"

She hung up before he came up with another daydream to pass off as the truth. Talking to him grew more pointless with each passing month. His skull had to be as thick as the delusions he harbored to keep from hating himself.

AFTER HIS MOTHER clicked the phone off, Eli did likewise. He set the extension on the desk, staring at the receiver. Feeling nothing.

Plenty of nothing. Which was worse than being sad. Maybe it was the biggest sadness.

He left even Lucy behind as he stumbled to the door. He had to go.

Outside. Somewhere. Had to find more darkness than the closet or the blanket.

At the top of the stairs, he stopped, surprised to see the open front door. Static had cut in and out on his mom's side of her talk with his dad. She'd been outside, trying to hide the truth about his father.

He'd always known. Some place inside him that held on to all the sadness he couldn't stop feeling.

At the door, he searched from side to side.

She wasn't there. He ran down the porch stairs and headed down the driveway. The woods. Bushes and flowers and stuff. Plenty of places to crawl inside.

But he turned the curve in the driveway and heard keyboard keys, clicking fast.

Aidan was typing away on his laptop on the cottage porch. Right beside him, he had a glass of something that made Eli lick his lips. He'd never been more thirsty.

"Hey, Aidan."

"Hey." He stood up. No smile. He didn't want company, either.

Tears twisted Eli's gut. Men didn't cry.

His own father hated him, never wanted to see him. It just piled up and piled up, hurting. And now his dad wouldn't even help with the one thing he wanted most. Eli couldn't see an end to his problems.

"What brings you down here?" Aidan asked.

"I don't know." He swallowed. It was hard to do. "What are you doing?"

"Work." He crossed his arms. "So I can't talk long. Did you tell your mother you were coming?"

The equivalent of "go talk to your mom." The same thing his dad always said. Aidan kicked a pile of gravel. He drove everyone he liked away. No one wanted him around anymore but his mom.

"Eli? What's wrong?"

"Nothing." He plastered a big smile on his face and backed away from the porch, giving the glass whose outside was speckled with water one last look. "I'm going to play in the woods."

"Do you have friends coming?"

"No."

"Call someone."

"Now you sound like my mom."

Eli ran through the gravel, snickering as it flew up from his heels. With any luck, it'd fly up onto the porch and hit that guy's laptop.

He ran into the woods.

WHAT KIND OF MAN chased a needy kid away—even when that was what his mother wanted? Aidan lasted about ten more minutes at his laptop before he shut the lid, cursing.

Beth was wrong. If Eli needed company, he couldn't turn the boy away. He wasn't crying wolf. He needed help, and a few minutes of Aidan's time wouldn't hurt him or break Nikolas Enterprises.

He followed Eli's path through the woods. Even since he'd arrived in Honesty, the weather had warmed and the plants filled out. The shrubbery seemed to close in, bunching up to keep out intruders.

A sudden crack stopped him. Another pellet gun?

A groan got him moving again.

He found the clearing quickly. To his horror, he also found Eli on the ground, a broken branch looped with his leather belt beside him. The other end of his belt was around his neck.

Two tarnished letters emblazoned the buckle, CT. It was his father's belt and plenty long enough to strangle him if that branch had been long and strong enough.

"Eli." He dropped to his knees, staring at the boy's blue face. The cold, wet ground penetrated when no thought would come.

Eli's chest was still. So still he reminded Aidan of Madeline.

Not again. Not again.

"Son?" He tilted the boy's head back—gently. What did a broken neck look like? "No one else dies on me, Eli, so you'd better start breathing."

The child's airway was clear. Aidan started CPR.

As he stopped breathing to apply pressure to Eli's chest, he yanked his phone out of his pocket and dialed 911 before tucking it between his ear and shoulder.

An operator answered. He kept pumping. "Get an ambulance out to the cottage at 1544 Post Road. Tell them to listen for me yelling. A boy's tried to hang himself, and I'm giving him CPR."

Letting the phone drop, he breathed for Eli again. As he straightened to pump, he started yelling. Beth's name.

Again and again.

A woman screamed close by. He turned his head toward the sound. She couldn't see them yet through the damn trees, but she knew.

"Beth, over here."

He breathed again. Beth burst into the clearing, reminding him oddly of the night he'd first arrived.

With leaves in her hair and horror in her eyes, she ran at them, collapsing at her son's side, her face wet.

Aidan pushed her hands away. "His neck," he said, and started breathing again.

"Let me." She shoved at his shoulders. "Your heart."

He finished the breathing cycle before he answered. "I'll stop if I feel anything. Pick up my phone. See if anyone's still there."

She shook her head, staring at her son. "Make him breathe. Make him breathe!"

As if Eli heard her, his chest expanded, on its own.

"Eli?" Thank God. He leaned over the boy's face, praying for the warm whoosh of air moving out of his lungs.

"He did it again." Beth lay on the ground, curving her arm around her son's head. "Keep on, baby. Breathe some more." Her voice could not have been sweeter, more filled with kindness. "You have to live, buddy. Please want to live."

The small—too small—surely he'd never looked so small before—chest rose again.

"I think he's doing it. I'm going to the driveway, Beth. Make sure he doesn't stop." He picked up his phone. "Are you there?"

The woman who'd answered him before said hello again.

"I can give you details now. Is someone coming?"

"Yes, sir. An ambulance is on the way. Did I hear you say Eli is breathing on his own?"

"How did you know it was Eli?"

"Do you think anyone in this town doesn't know who lives at 1544 Post Road?"

"His mother's still with him. I'm going to wait by the driveway so they'll know where to stop."

"You left Beth alone?"

"I didn't want to leave either of them."

"HIS NECK IS FINE. Nothing broken." Brent looked up from the tests he'd run again. "I don't see anything in his bloodwork."

"How do you know? They took two days before." They stood outside the glass-fronted ICU room, but Beth couldn't take her eyes off her son who had an oxygen line in his nose and barely took up half the bed. A growing boy shouldn't look so tiny.

"This was an emergency. You saw Dr. Drayton? What did you think?"

She clenched her fingers around the counter. Brent had asked her out to the nurses' station to talk while the staff was busy with patients. "If you bring him over here, I'll tear him apart with my bare hands."

Brent had the decency to blush. "I thought he might be okay because he can come across as a father figure."

"Or a troll," Beth said.

"How about Dr. Lester?"

"I loved her. Eli thought she was too much like me."

"And that was bad?" He wrote something and glanced at his watch before making another note.

"According to Eli."

"Let me call Maria Keaton then." Brent tried to reach for the phone. It was too far away. "You can talk to her before she sees Eli. If you're dead set against her, we'll find another therapist, but we need to find someone soon."

Beth nodded, unable to think. She felt pain from head to toe, some crazy physical reaction to what had happened. She hated to think how Eli must feel, and she could do nothing for him.

At the end of the white-tiled hall, one of the double doors swung open. An orderly pushed a patient on a gurney through. Behind him, Aidan stood, his hands at his sides, still in a state of shock.

Beth ached for the man who'd saved her son's life. "Who will we find, Brent?" Aidan would know someone. He'd be able to drag some specialist from Timbuktu if Eli needed it.

"I don't know. Meet Maria and then we'll worry about what comes next."

"But is he going to be all right?" She shuddered in the hospital cold, grabbing her friend's sleeve, leaning hard on the counter to keep from falling.

"Physically, yes, but we have to keep him here for a few days. He needs constant supervision, and then we'll see what Maria says about psychotherapy. Sometimes, talk takes care of the problem if the therapist is capable, but I'd like to start Eli on an SSRI for the present. We can wean him off as he responds to treatment."

"SSRI?"

"A selective serotonin reuptake inhibitor. Basically, they make more serotonin available in the brain, which eases a patient's depression."

She dropped both hands on the Formica surface. "Eli's not just a patient. He's the boy you've known all his life. Don't you back away from him behind that patient talk."

"I wouldn't." He pulled her close across the counter and she felt better for a moment. "Sometimes I have to sound like a doctor."

She stepped back to search his face. "I've heard those drugs can cause suicidal feelings."

"They can help, too. Right now, I think we need to try them. The combination of meds and talk therapy often helps children. If Eli doesn't need the drug, or if he tells us the bad feelings are worse, we'll take him off."

"And this Dr. Keaton knows what she's doing?"

"She's probably the one I'd choose first."

"Then why did you put her last?" What if they were too late to help Eli?

"I didn't want to influence your decision." He hugged her again, one-armed. "Which makes me feel like an idiot. Let me call her."

"Okay." She looked toward those double doors

again. "I know Aidan isn't eligible to visit since he's not family, but he saved my son's life." She'd never forget the sight of him working desperately to breathe for Eli.

She pressed one fist into her impossibly tight chest. If she had any courage she'd admit she also needed Aidan's compassion. She just wanted him near.

"I'll bring him in later. Right now, you're enough for Eli."

She nodded. Pushing away from the counter, she flattened her hand on the glass door to open it. A chair stood in the corner. Beth lifted it and then set it down close to Eli's bed.

Perching on the hard seat, she folded her son's hand between her own. His felt cold and unresponsive.

They'd given him something to make him sleep because he'd started crying and couldn't stop on the way to the hospital. Beth pressed her cheek to their hands and breathed in the scent of uber-clean sheets.

She closed her eyes. The better to pretend she wasn't crying, too.

"MRS. TULLY?"

She looked up, blinking because her eyes were swollen and dry. A young girl stood in front of her wearing a skirt about as wide as a seat belt and a snug-fitting T-shirt. With her hair in a loose knot, she looked about sixteen.

But she had knowledge in her eyes—and sympathy without the sour flavor of pity.

"I'm Dr. Keaton." She shook Beth's hand. "Would you like to step outside for a moment?"

Beth's gaze snapped to Eli. He looked the same. A small frown drew the faintest line on his forehead. "Is something else wrong with my son?"

"I'm the psychologist Dr. Brent suggested. You were supposed to meet with me on Monday."

"I know." Beth nodded, reluctant to leave Eli alone. "You sounded concerned. I thought something might have happened while I was asleep."

"No problem. Could we go as far as the hall? You'll be able to see him."

"Okay."

Dr. Keaton held the door and then closed it firmly. "I hope you won't think I'm rude, but I suggest you see someone, too, Mrs. Tully. You're in shock."

"When my son doesn't need me." Beth searched for her spirit. Normally, such a suggestion would have insulted her. "Brent told you what happened?"

"Yes, when he called."

"How old are you?" Beth straightened her own shirt. "I'm sorry for being rude, but you look too young to help anyone, and I can't handle any more—trouble—Dr. Keaton."

"You can keep calling me that if you like. I use it to make patients and their families remember I've finished my training and been in practice for nearly ten years. I'm probably older than you, and my name is Maria. I have excellent credentials, which I'm happy to share with you. Brent says you've turned down his other two options?"

Maria Keaton might look like someone's baby sister, but she sounded calm and certain. She gave Beth a sense of hope.

And Beth could imagine Maria, right at home on a skateboard.

"I'd like you to try with Eli as long as he's happy with you after he wakes up."

"The E.R. physician—" Dr. Keaton looked at her palm, on which something was written in blue ink "—Dr. Galt, tells me he gave Eli a sedative, but your son should wake soon. He's going to be fine."

"Fine?" Beth tried not to overreact. Calm was one thing. Too much confidence could only hurt her son. "He tried to kill himself. Failing won't make him less eager to do it."

"We'll soon find out why and we'll give him safer tools to handle the things that bother him." Dr. Keaton reached into her back skirt pocket and tugged out a stack of business cards. She flipped through a few before she pulled one out. "My numbers are on there, Mrs. Tully. If you want to talk, I'm available any time of the day or night. You matter to me as much as Eli because you'll be part of his getting well."

"You don't sound a lot like the other doctors."

"I'm glad." Her smile was as serene as a prayer. "And you look like the younger sister I never had."

"I can help your son, and I have no rules other

than ethics, so I'll try whatever he needs. I once had a breakthrough with someone your age on a climbing wall." She swished her ponytail over her shoulder. "Scared the crap out of me, but my patient faced her whole life as we went over the top."

Beth had never coped well with arrogant people, and the doctor was, in a strange, kind way. "What happens next?"

"When Eli wakes, I'll introduce myself and ask if he wants to talk about anything. I'll tell him I've informed the hospital staff they're to call me the second he needs me for any reason, and we'll start building trust in each other. Mrs. Tully, you're staring at me."

"My name is Beth." She blinked. "I'm praying you're as good as you believe, and that I'll be able to make myself let you take care of Eli without interfering. My son's life depends on you."

"And on you, and on all his friends. Does he have a pet?"

"A dog, Lucy. He loves her," Beth said. "More than anything."

"Maybe you could bring her to the parking lot and let him look out the window at her."

"Just say when." Maybe it would be all right. Maria's confidence rubbed off.

"Try not to worry, Beth. Think of me as being the next doctor in the line. If I don't work out, you can keep on shopping."

The door to the hall popped open again and

again, Beth saw Aidan. He was staring at the short-skirted doctor at her side.

"Maria."

"I thought I'd see you in a hospital at some point, Aidan." She looked at Beth. "Friend of yours?"

CHAPTER ELEVEN

BETH FELT as if she were being sucked down a drain. She pitched her voice low. "You didn't try to help his wife?"

"I worked for his company after she died."

Beth searched Aidan's face for the kind of horror she'd feel if—something—happened to Eli in this woman's care. There was none. Just surprise.

The door closed on him again.

"How did you get here?" Beth asked Maria.

"He fired me. I didn't fit in with the pinstripe and PDA crowd."

Beth tried to speak.

"You're rethinking." Maria nodded. "And that's fine, but I'm perfect for a skateboarding teen. I suggest people don't take themselves so seriously. Imagine how that erodes an executive's ego."

"How do you know Eli skateboards?"

"Your son almost died tonight. When Brent called to ask me if I'd see him I found out everything I could. Brent faxed me his notes, and I made a few calls."

"Okay." She started to add that they'd give it a try, but Eli moved on his bed. His mouth formed the word *Mom*.

The door thudded beneath her hands. She skidded to his side. He opened his eyes and looked around the room, exposing the bruises at his throat.

"Eli—" Her voice gave out. Her son stared at her, his face pure yearning.

"I'm sorry." His tone rasped.

Sorry? Startling herself, she got angry—because she saw a chance for him to be okay, and the thought of life without him made her furious. "It's okay." She put her hand on the top of his head and held on to his hair, afraid to touch anywhere else. His arms weakly held her, and she kissed his forehead. "We'll figure it out."

"You're awake, Eli. I'm glad."

Beth turned. "Aidan?"

He came to the bed and put one arm around her waist. His smile for Eli was pure relief. Eli beamed back, holding his throat because it must hurt.

"I told Maria you both mattered to me," Aidan said. "She got me in."

ELI HAD FALLEN ASLEEP again. Only his breathing made any sound in the room. Aidan glanced at Beth. They'd shared over an hour watching her son's chest rise and fall.

He couldn't forget one of his first thoughts on seeing Eli had been "Not again." His guilt over his ex-wife's death had brought on a heart attack. He couldn't be sure he'd recovered enough to take on a real family, based on love, rather than their need of his help. He didn't trust himself to know the difference.

As he reached the glass door, he saw Van in the hall. Beth's brother waited, clearly troubled to see him.

"What are you doing here?" he asked.

The door behind them opened again. "Van," Beth said, "Aidan saved Eli's life, and he's my friend."

"Your friend?" Questions passed between brother and sister, but Aidan, used to reading nuance, didn't understand. His senses seemed to be deserting him.

"You should thank him," Beth said.

"I came back to see Eli." He glanced at Aidan again. "And maybe I should stay."

"Stay as long as you want. Eli could use your company. He told me he heard me talking to Campbell just before he…" She couldn't put Eli's suicide attempt into words. Van hugged her tight. "He heard Campbell making the usual excuses, and they weren't believable. He saw the truth."

"I'll get that coffee," Aidan said. "Would you like a cup, Van?"

"You don't have to wait on us."

"I'm going anyway." These two. You couldn't do them the smallest favor.

"Thanks, then." Van stuck out his hand. "And thanks for saving my nephew."

Aidan shook his hand. No man could react normally after his nephew had tried to kill himself.

"What have you been doing to that guy?" Van asked Beth as Aidan headed for the break room the nurses had shown them.

He wanted to look back. Beth's whispered response was inaudible, but annoyed. He'd give a lot to know what she'd said.

AFTER A TAP AT THE DOOR, Campbell swung into the room, natty in gabardine khakis and a linen shirt. He'd gone to seed. An affection for fast food had given him both bad skin and a bit of a belly, and Beth couldn't help rejoicing in both because his appearance and his fun had always mattered more than Eli.

She walked to the window. They'd moved Eli to a regular room after Maria suggested he felt like an insect.

"Dad." Eli's happiness almost made Campbell's visit bearable. Reflected in the glass, he opened his arms wide. His father went in for a minihug and then straightened.

"I can't believe you're in here, son. What happened?"

"What do you mean?" Their child, eleven going on a hundred, seemed to expect something different than Campbell's usual used-car-salesman patter. "It was—after I heard you talking to Mom."

"You did all this over a skateboard?" His dad

strolled to the end of the bed. "Beth, why didn't you just give him the skateboard?"

Beth turned on him, ready to attack. "Maybe you think you're joking. You may even think Eli can be teased out of his 'funk,' but this is different, Campbell."

"What are you talking about?"

"Stop, Campbell. We don't need to argue about this right now. What you have to do is be a father to our son. Either be an adult and buckle down or get out of here."

"Mom?"

"Don't worry, Eli. I'm not telling him to leave. I want him to stay. I just don't want him to hurt you and pretend you don't need help."

"Nice, in front of the boy."

"He has to know someone puts him first," she said.

"Dad, please stop."

"Son, it's no big deal. I'm sure everyone misunderstood what you did. Tell them. You just want a skateboard. They'll let you out of here."

As straws went, it weighed about a hundred tons. Beth turned and walked toward him, deliberately keeping her face averted from Eli.

"You need to leave, Campbell, and you are not to see my son until I think you're fit to."

"Eah?"

"I don't know what that sound means, but you'd better go."

"I should have visited sooner, but I don't know what to say to sick people, and he looks fine to me.

I believe things got out of hand. Let's call it even. I'm a father who waits too long to do the right thing, and Eli really wanted that toy."

"You're a father who wouldn't know the right thing if it ran you down, and Eli isn't capable of pretending to be ill. You don't even know him. Now leave this room, and don't go near my brother's house or mine when it's rebuilt. I'll call you when I think Eli's well enough to deal with your deliberate obtuseness."

"Does that mean when he pretends he doesn't understand?" Eli asked.

"Exactly."

"Son—" Campbell gaped at them. "Do you really want me to leave? You want to see me, don't you?"

"No," Eli said. "Go away."

"I can't—" Then to Beth "—You'll be sorry."

"I don't see how." The sheer relief of knowing he couldn't make Eli worse was worth the fight.

Campbell barely swung back out of the room with tattered style before a nurse came in. "Mr. Nikolas is here," she said. She patted Eli's pillow. "You want to see him?"

"Yeah," Eli said.

"Can you give us a second?" Beth ignored how her pulse began to stutter at the mention of Aidan's name.

"Let me know when you're ready," the nurse said, glossing over the room's tension.

After she shut the door, Beth sat on Eli's bed. "Are you okay?"

"Why doesn't Dad love me?"

"He does. He's just a huge kid who loves himself most." She threaded her fingers together and squeezed so hard it hurt. "I don't know a lot about him anymore, but I won't let him come near you again until he changes. If he's able."

"You pretended he was a good guy except for that time you made the cops arrest him."

"I didn't want to make you think you couldn't trust your father when you didn't trust me."

"I get that, but don't do it again." He hugged her. His small arms felt so good. "I always trusted you, Mom, but Dad ignores me when I'm mad at him, and you at least try to talk to me."

"So all your irritation has been affection, huh?"

"Yeah. Cut out the crying, though."

"The nurse said I could interrupt." Aidan came in holding out his phone for Eli, raking Beth with concern.

She shook her head, managing a watery smile. He turned back to her son.

"I brought pictures. This morning Lucy wandered down to the house so I took her for a run." He leaned down to show Eli, and Beth wanted to curl up between them.

"Thanks, Aidan." Eli started flipping through the photos, his face happy.

Why couldn't his own father have done something so small and yet so kind?

A FEW DAYS LATER, Beth and Maria shared tasty coffee in Maria's office.

"Beth, I think the camp would do Eli a lot of good. He'll learn about camping and hiking and climbing. He'll be with other children who share many of his feelings. He won't be the odd man out."

"Is it my fault? Is that why you want to send him away? Dr. Drayton said as much, because I hover and, apparently, I'm not manly enough to be a dad for Eli, too."

"Dr. Drayton can have funny ideas." She plucked a Kleenex from a box on her serviceable cherry laminate desk. Unlike Dr. Lester, she hadn't built a cozy nest. Unlike Dr. Drayton, she didn't need a men's club. "Only his assumptions aren't that funny if you're the butt of them. Ignore it. You know you're doing your best with Eli. You can't take his father's place because he has a father."

"I married Campbell when I was too young to really know him, and then we went to Florida with his grandparents for almost a year. I had to depend on him." Beth blew her nose and cursed her own weakness. Was she equally blind when she looked at Aidan? "Maybe I convinced myself he was decent, but the older Eli gets, the less he can depend on Campbell."

"Are you angry with your ex-husband, or with yourself?"

"Do I have to choose?"

"I'm not excusing him, but he might be afraid.

Maybe he's been hiding behind fear since you were children. It can freeze some people."

"He doesn't get off that easy. Do you think he's as scared as Eli was when he climbed that tree?" She shuddered at the too-vivid image.

Maria pushed a pencil across her glass blotter. "Eli is finally facing the truth about him. That's what matters to us. Your brother came home for a couple of days, and I notice Aidan visits every day. Eli has other grown males in his life."

"Yeah." Beth was careful. Not even Aidan could guess how relieved she was each time he walked into the room. He'd stayed another day and another, but the days would eventually run out.

"You don't want to talk about Aidan?"

"You're not my doctor." She evaded Maria's glance. The woman was too damn smart. "We should discuss Eli's trip. Visiting hours start soon, and I have to find the money to pay for his treatment." She didn't care if her spreadsheets and careful budget spontaneously combusted. If she had to, she'd ask Van for help.

"WHY CAN'T I stay here?" Eli almost hated his mom for trying to send him away. Maria was pretty and nice and he liked her a lot. He liked the way she saw stuff.

"Maria suggested the camp, Eli. She says it'll be a good step for you."

What the hell? "I'm not scared of those kids at school."

"The camp has teachers for you. They'll get a copy of your transcript from school and notes from all your other teachers about your progress. You can finish the year up, and next fall, you'll be back with your old friends."

Like a little bit of heaven. He took refuge in their usual problems. "Can we afford this place? Camping costs money, and I don't have equipment."

His mother's mouth trembled. Her lie look. She thought she was the best at keeping stuff from him, but he always knew. "I'll find the money even if I have to ask Uncle Van for a loan. Insurance helps," she said.

Insurance. Hell. She thought he was stupid.

In his mind, he saw himself throwing the huge cup of water at the window. That scared him—it was how he'd ended up hanging from that tree. He'd imagined the quiet and the darkness of being—"You couldn't find a cheaper way to get rid of me?"

His mother's mouth dropped. He'd never seen anyone actually do that.

"You're mad at me," she said, as if he'd invented something as cool as a brand-new skateboard. "Ever since you saw me that first night, you've acted scared and sad, and you keep apologizing, but you're mad at me again."

"Wouldn't you be? You think I'm going to hurt myself again, but I won't." He'd told Maria the truth. A second too late, he'd known he didn't want to die.

He couldn't say that to his mom yet.

She ran her hand down the sheet, like she used to pat his arm or his shoulder. "If I could, I'd come with you. I'd carry you up the mountains. I'd climb with you on my back."

"I know that." He almost laughed, but she wanted to send him away. She didn't get to know he could laugh again. He looked out the window. All the trees were green. And they blocked most of the sky.

"You know I'd never 'get rid' of you?"

"You keep trying to get rid of my friends. Where's Aidan?"

Her face turned bright red. "He's better, too. You know he's going home soon."

"I'm not the one who's falling for him." Half joking, he was surprised when she turned even redder. "You really do like him," he said.

"Don't you?"

"Not like that." He grabbed the blanket on his bed. Not content to run his friends out of town, she had to horn in and try to take them.

A knock at the door, and Aidan came in. "I brought you a visitor, Eli."

Trying to hide how mad he was, Eli looked past him. "Who?" Probably some jerk from school.

Aidan had eyes only for Eli's mom.

He'd never looked at Eli as if he expected him to jump off the nearest bridge, but he wasn't supposed to look at his mom, either.

"We have to go downstairs. I stopped in to ask Maria, and she said I could take you down."

Eli bolted out of bed. "You are my friend," he said, looking for his flip-flops. "You brought Lucy."

"You did what?" his mom asked. Her voice stopped him halfway into his shoes. She wasn't breathing and her eyes—she looked at Aidan the way women in movies looked at the guy in charge.

"I told Mrs. Carleton I was taking her," he said.

"Thank you." His mother put her hand on Aidan's shoulder, and "thank you" sounded like something Eli wasn't supposed to hear.

Aidan covered her hand. No one had ever stared at her like that. Eli turned away and then remembered he'd been putting on his shoes.

"Let's go," Aidan said. "An orderly's holding her for me, and he probably has other work to do."

Eli ignored them, running ahead to the elevator. They barely made it before the doors slid shut. He would have gone downstairs without them.

"What's going on?" Aidan asked. "Did I interrupt something?"

Yeah. His whole life. Not that he wanted his mom and dad back together any more. "No," he said, and his mother said it at almost the same time.

When the elevator opened, he ran for the doors. Lucy must have smelled him coming. She started jumping and the orderly backed as far away as her leash would let him.

"She doesn't hurt anyone." He tore around the doors and grabbed her with a quick thanks. Laughing, Eli buried his face in his dog's black coat.

But this time, when darkness covered him, he snapped his head up, breathing hard.

The dark scared him now.

AIDAN CAUGHT Beth's arm as Eli bolted across the driveway to a park the hospital had built for its ambulatory patients. Lucy galloped at his side.

"What's wrong with him?"

"Me, his idiot father and he doesn't want to go to camp."

"There's more." She didn't elaborate. He went on. "I'm being pushy again, but I looked up the camp online and I found some photos other kids took there. Do you think he'd like to see them?"

"I shouldn't even let you talk to him. When are you leaving, Aidan?"

"Will you listen to me? I won't let him down. As long as he needs me, he can count on me."

"Why?"

"How can you ask? I helped him start breathing again. I watched him suffer for his dog as if he were her dad and she was his baby. I see him in pain, and I have to help. And he's your son, Beth. How could I not care enough to be his friend?"

She eyed him too carefully, then took a deep breath. "I owe you everything so I'm trying to believe, but we're people you met on a trip away from home. How long until some broken-winged company takes our place on your to-do list?"

"I'm tired of you dismissing me." He didn't reach

out to every woman and child he met. Yet, why set Eli's recovery back, arguing with his mom in the parking lot? "I'll get the pictures and meet you."

Beth put her head down, but kept walking. The pavement's heat seeped through the soles of his shoes as he watched her go.

A warning whispered. Don't start thinking of this kid as a son with Beth waiting for him to run out of her and Eli's lives.

He opened his car and took out the photos he'd printed that morning. By the time he caught up with the most difficult woman in his world and the boy who made him want to learn how to be a father, Eli was throwing a stick for Lucy. Beth had taken a vigilant seat on a bench.

"Eli," he said, "I found pictures of The Falcon's Nest. Other kids who've gone up there posted them on the Web."

"Yeah?" He glanced over, but suddenly, he didn't seem so happy to see Aidan.

"Don't you want to take a look?" Beth asked.

He held out his hand. Aidan handed them over and then started to join Beth on the bench, but she stood as soon as he came near. "Can I see them, too?" she asked.

When she reached Eli, he shoved the pictures at her. "Lucy," he said, "let's get you some water."

"Wait," Beth said, "couldn't we talk about the camp?"

"I know about it. Maria told me and you told me.

It'll build my self-confidence. I'll have school, and a psychologist will talk to me once a day—check on me—and I'll climb mountains."

"Not really mountains," Beth said, and Aidan wished he could put his arms around her and promise everything would be all right.

"Look at the pictures," he said instead. "The other children are having fun."

Eli turned, quivering with rage. Relief flooded Aidan, its intensity surprising him. The boy had found his emotions. The only thing Madeline had ever felt was abandoned. Aidan hid his happiness even as Eli tried to skewer him on a glance rich with fury.

"Why don't you go?" Eli asked. "Instead of helping my mom get rid of me—so you can be with her—why don't you go?"

Lucy stood up and barked.

"It might be time I did that," Aidan said.

Beth didn't seem surprised. He wanted to explain. To tell her he was just getting out of Eli's way, but how could he stay when Eli was looking for a weapon?

TAKING HER CHILD to the bus to meet the other campers was the hardest thing Beth had ever done. The previous afternoon, he'd come home from the hospital. They'd spent a silent shopping day, stocking up on his supplies. They'd shared a silent dinner, and then Beth had sat a silent vigil at her barely open bedroom door, listening for any sound.

The next morning, as she drooled on her shirt, with her head lodged in a corner between the wall and her bureau, Eli slept in. When he woke, she slammed her head into the dresser, pretended she hadn't slept on the floor and joined him to grab an energy bar and some juice for breakfast.

Sleeping well was a good sign. Unless he'd slept too well. Couldn't that also be a sign of depression?

No wonder she was driving him crazy. They packed all his new gear, and she made him have lunch.

"Let's load your stuff in the car," she said after she washed the glasses from their meager meal.

The bus waited in the hospital parking lot. Children, both boys and girls, ranging in age from eight to eleven, stowed their things in the open storage bin. The kids said goodbye to their parents with varying degrees of reluctance. One little girl was crying so hard, Beth teared up.

Eli remained stoic until the last minute. He was on the bus before he turned and pushed his way past a kid who shoved him back as he tried to climb down.

"Bye, Mom." He hugged her. "I'll be all right. I'm not ever going to hurt myself again. I told Maria, but I want you to know, too."

"How can you be sure?" she asked, her throat constricted.

"At the last minute, I changed my mind. I won't ever forget that feeling. You can't help thinking of me as a kid, but I'll show you. Gotta go."

He turned, but she pulled him back, picturing him leading a pack of troubled children up Everest. "You don't have to show me anything."

"I'm not going to fall off one of those hills."

He knew her too well. "I'll see you in two weeks," she said, "as soon as I can visit."

"Yeah." He pulled his arm free. "I gotta go. The other kids are watching out the windows. What do you expect, a dance?"

Beth laughed. He laughed, too, looking a little startled. Then he ran to the bus, the last one to climb on. A woman wearing a Falcon's Nest T-shirt followed him up the stairs, glancing back. She flashed Beth an *okay* sign just before the doors closed, and the bus started.

Beth squinted into the sunny sky and watched the bus weave through the parking lot. As it turned down the street, she shook her head.

Dangling off a mountain was supposed to make Eli well. Letting him go was pretty much the same therapy for her.

CHAPTER TWELVE

"Wow, Josh." Dazed, Beth stared at the bones of her new home. Josh, the roofer, had started with his crew that day. She'd spent the afternoon distracting herself with errands she'd been putting off. After Eli had reached the camp, he'd sent her a text message to say they'd arrived. Suddenly she'd had to look at the lodge before she went back to Van's. "It looks like a house again."

"When were you here last?"

"Over a week ago, just before they started framing."

"Yeah, I was sorry to hear about Eli."

"Thanks." In the warmth of spring, with a breeze caressing her face and the clear sky a theater of early evening beauty, Beth thought back to her son's hospital bedside, and she didn't trust herself to talk about it. "They framed the house in a week?"

"With a big crew, it goes fast."

"How long will you all take?"

"Another two weeks, maybe. Depends on the weather."

"Doesn't it always?"

And that was all the conversation Beth could make. Her mind was on Eli and only Eli. Was he okay? Afraid on his own?

Relieved to be out of her reach?

"Don't worry about a thing, Mrs. Tully. You'll have this roof for another twenty, maybe thirty years."

"Thanks, Josh." She tried not to mind a kid probably six years younger than she calling her Mrs. Tully. "I'll get out of your way. I guess you're packing up to go home?"

"Yeah. I stayed a little longer than usual tonight. I meant to get an earlier start this morning, so I let the other guys go and did a little more."

"Don't get hurt."

"Okay."

Eli used that same tone to agree and shut her up all at the same time. Since she had no desire to eventually put her roofer on a bus out of town, she decided not to mother him in the absence of her son. "Talk to you later. You have my cell number if you need to reach me?"

"Sure."

She pointed to the ladder lying on the ground beside him. "Do you need help?"

"I'm golden."

"See you, then." She headed back to her car. Home would be empty, unless Mrs. Carleton had found extra tasks. Van had returned to his business meetings after the doctors assured them Eli would do best at camp.

She drove to the park in town and turned in to the same parking spot she'd used when Eli was a small child. He'd loved to come here and run through the fountain that squirted out of the cobbled labyrinth. After, he'd dry out while she'd pushed him on one of the chain swings.

"Higher, Mommy, higher."

Another boy's voice drew Beth to the picket fence that hugged the park and protected the children from running into the baseball fields or the busy street. The little guy kicked his feet into the air as his mom pushed him, chatting with her friend whose daughter was on the next swing.

Beth closed her hands on two pickets and leaned back, looking up at the sky. Only a trace of sunlight still veined the dark blue.

"Beth?"

She turned so fast she drove a splinter into her palm. "Aidan." She turned up her hand and tried to pull out the sliver.

"Let me help you. I didn't mean to startle you."

"I can do it."

"I know you can, but do you have to?"

She pulled back, ignoring his pointed question. "I should have called you before now." They hadn't seen him since Eli'd been so aggressive.

"I understood. How is he?"

"I don't know." She pulled out the splinter and

blamed her swelling heart on the almost-nothing-pain. "He's gone to camp. He was allowed to text me when he arrived, so all I know is that he's there."

"What if he didn't have a cell?"

"He'd get to call on one of their pay phones." She pressed her hands together to ease the sting and whipped up a smile. "Maybe I should have tossed his cell into the lake on the way over here."

He grinned. God, the man was beautiful. And he'd been kind. He deserved better than her and Eli's testy mistrust. He couldn't help that she'd grown used to turning to him when she was afraid.

"What is it, Beth? Why are you so sad?"

Around them the night flowed into town, and the children laughed and regret reached delicate fingers to make her shiver. "I'm sorry I can't know you better."

All the lines in his face sobered. "I've never said you couldn't."

"You're leaving. You were the perfect choice for Eli's father figure until he thought I was starting to care for you. Now he doesn't want you around. Even if I believed in you or me or the future, how could I make his problems worse?"

"I'm not going anywhere, and whatever Eli thinks about you and me together, we'll deal with it."

"Be serious, Aidan. I believe you'd never hurt Eli or me on purpose, and I don't think you're lying, but you are making promises you can't keep."

He grabbed one of the pickets. His eyes were on

the swing sets, but he didn't seem to see anything until he faced her again. "What do you know that I don't, Beth? Why are you so determined not to get involved?"

"I'm scared for my son. And for me."

"It's too late. We started mattering to each other the second you ran through that hedge."

"Forget that living in a town like this would bore you out of your wits, and I won't move Eli. Ever. You have a business that needs you in D.C." She shook her head, so that her hair flew into her eyes as she started walking toward her car. "What am I even talking about? None of this matters because you and I are an impossibility."

"That's not a word." He came up behind her. "I can't promise forever, but neither can you. We have to see what comes next."

"What comes next for me is getting my son well." Her car felt too far away. She walked fast, swatting at grass that tickled her ankles, but then she stopped so abruptly he bumped into her. Splaying her hands on his chest, she pushed away and wondered if she'd ever forget the beat of his heart against her palm. "I'm not sure I thanked you."

"You have," he said, "and you never needed to."

"I have to balance accounts between us."

"Eli told me once that you try to pretend you're not as nice as you are. He says you do it for protection."

"He was wrong."

AIDAN TRIED TO LET HER GO. He stopped where she left him and let her open her car door before he yelled, "Hey!" All around them, people turned. People who knew Beth and would talk about the crazy man yelling at her in the park.

Too bad.

He ran to her. She met him, waving her hands in a slow-down gesture.

"Are you allowed to run?"

"I told you I'm not going to die, Beth."

"Well, don't."

"Let me talk to you. You're afraid—just like your son. I know how that feels, but there's more to survival than taking the next breath."

"Not now. Maybe not ever if Eli doesn't want you around."

"MRS. CARLETON?" Beth set her keys and purse on the kitchen counter. Mrs. Carleton didn't answer.

What a day of firsts. For her soul's sake, she needed to take care of her son, but she'd sent him away to strangers. At the lodge, she'd found the framing up and the roof started. She should be happier, but it only mattered because it was Eli's home.

She'd run like a frightened sheep from the one man she might be able to love. And she wasn't absolutely sure why. He'd given her no reason to believe him a liar. She just couldn't make herself accept he was telling the truth, and she wouldn't risk upsetting Eli.

And now, she wished Mrs. Carleton were still here. She would have reminded Beth that her duty lay in this house, not in the cottage down the hill.

Beth flipped open her cell phone and called Van. "I'm sorry, but I have to hurry. What's up?"

"Not enough to keep you on the phone. I'm lonely. Eli's gone and I can't talk to him for two weeks."

"They can't stop you."

"I agreed when I let him go to the camp."

"Maybe you both need the break."

Way to parrot Maria Keaton. "I won't keep you." Or beg him to talk her out of doing anything crazy tonight—like knocking on the cottage door.

"Thanks for letting me know where Eli is. Call back later if you want to talk, okay?"

Later might be too late. "Okay, Van." She hung up and considered calling Campbell, but her heart froze. He didn't deserve it. If he wanted information, he could work for it. She'd made it too easy for him to neglect their son. She was always in the middle, trying to build a relationship between them.

She stuffed the phone back in her pocket in case Eli somehow called.

Maybe a bite to eat?

The kitchen was clean. Beth missed Eli's laughter, the way he tempted Lucy with a bite of bacon or a sliver of fish.

A thump overhead startled her. Then paws clicked along the hallway and down the stairs.

"Lucy?"

The dog whined as she came. Beth poured food into her bowl and gave her fresh water. Lucy sat, not eating.

"I didn't want him to go," Beth said. "And defending myself to you may be ridiculous." She reached for the leash. "Want to go for a walk?"

If Eli asked, their easygoing dog slipped into a frenzy. Tonight, Lucy slid to the floor and rested her nose on her paws.

"Okay," Beth said. "I'll go by myself. And don't you be wishing those kids with the pellet guns on me."

She shut the door and wandered down the driveway. Like Eli, she couldn't help searching Aidan's porch in the hope he'd be there. He was.

She stopped, and stopped breathing, too.

He stood. "I hoped you'd come."

"I'm walking. Lucy refused to come, so I'm walking alone."

"You could walk with me."

And she could opt to believe neither of them meant anything deeper than the words they were mouthing.

"No," she said.

"Come in, Beth."

"I can't."

"It's easy. You walk up the path, climb the steps and I'll take your hands and pull you the rest of the way."

"That's not easy. I know what lies at the end of this path."

"It could be happiness."

"I haven't been that lucky."

"Beth." His disappointment seduced her more than his invitation. "One of the things I like best about you is your inability to give in when life smacks you around."

"Aww, that's nice. Most people say I'm too hardheaded."

"Then come to me and find out if there really is safety in numbers."

She didn't want to go in, and she didn't want to leave. If only Van would call back now. "I could pretend I don't know what's happening."

He shook his head. "Not you."

"You get to the heart of a deal."

Twisting his mouth, he shrugged.

"What kind of woman am I, wanting to be with you when I can only think of my son?"

"You're a woman whose son lived, despite his best efforts. You're one of the luckiest women on earth, but you're human. You love your son and your mind is filled with him, but your body wants a connection and comfort."

"Is that what the kids are calling it these days?"

Aidan's laugh was as sexy as the casual stride that brought him down the steps. "You want me." He stopped in front of her, and she felt his need to touch her. When she thought she might scream if he didn't, he pointed one long finger and pushed her hair over her shoulder. He leaned closer and breathed in.

"From the moment I met you, I've loved your scent, but it makes me hungry for you."

A sound, deep in her throat, vaguely shamed her. His husky voice worked like foreplay. The man sounded as if he cared. She must have felt that early in her marriage—before her marriage, maybe—but the care of a good man had been sadly lacking in her life.

"I'm not asking you to forget Eli. We'll talk about him later, but for now, think of you and me," Aidan said. "Feel how good it is to touch me because I don't want to let you go. Is it good, Beth?" His lips brushed her throat, up and down, up and down, back and forth. Feather-soft, his touch left her longing. She slid her hands over his shoulders and held on.

"This can't be right."

"It feels right."

She shook her head. He pushed her hair out of his way again, with his nose, as his mouth chased gooseflesh across her skin.

"Does the camp have your cell number?"

Her shivers punctuated every word he spoke against her. "Yes."

"Could you do anything for Eli if you went and sat outside the gates?"

"He's my baby. He needs me."

"He's not a baby." Aidan closed his hands around her waist and forced her to meet his eyes. "He may be young in years, but that's all."

"Which makes this worse. I let him down."

"The people are trained to offer the help he'll need."

"What if he thinks I don't love him?"

Aidan didn't answer, but his eyes seemed to grow moist. He shook his head as if he were choking. She tightened her fingers on his shoulders. "I'm sorry," she said, remembering too late that Madeline had chosen to die because she'd never believed Aidan loved her. "I'm so sorry."

He looked into her eyes, his grief as deep and troubled as her own. Maybe he was right. For one night, couldn't they stop thinking? Couldn't she be with this man who made her remember she was a woman and alive?

She eased his head down until their mouths met and clung. He opened his lips. She sank against him, fumbling in the darkness of need, of not knowing how to help him, of never having been with any man except Campbell, and feeling sure she must have lost all her good sense.

He slid his hands down her back again. She warmed and weakened, and she clung to him. He hugged back. They were two bodies, yearning for more than a glimpse of closeness that neither had felt before.

"Come inside?" he asked again.

"If I don't, we're going to put on a show for those neighbor kids."

"Surely they have bedtimes."

"Aidan, it's now or never. We can't talk about

boys or curfews. If I remember Eli threw you off the hospital grounds, I'll never be able to—"

He kissed her, backing toward the porch. Beth went along, tripped once and steadied herself with his strength. He let her go when they reached the steps, and she ran up them beside him.

At the door, he took her in his arms again and they stumbled inside. He shut the door, and the silence overtook need that had been inescapable.

"Oh, no," she said. Just to be human tonight, to give in to temptation that would taunt her for the rest of her life if she didn't spend one night with this man who made her want him.

"Don't," he said. "I wasn't lying when I told Maria I cared about you and Eli. I have the staying power to make him see I'm not coming between you."

"That's too much confession. We're about to—"

He nodded with wicked, sexy eyes. "But you don't want promises?"

"I've never made love without them." She grimaced. "They weren't true."

Silence came back into the room. Now was not the time to list her former husband's failings. If Eli didn't want Aidan in their lives as anything more than his computer-game friend, she couldn't let Aidan think she was dreaming of a future.

"What?" Aidan said. Maybe he was offering her freedom. She could say right now that Eli was too big a problem to overcome.

"I've never heard that clock tick before," Beth

said instead. "It must have been here. It belonged to my grandmother, but I've never heard it—"

He cut her off with a kiss that made her forget about clocks and grandmothers and bad emotional risks. His hands slipped beneath her shirt. She groaned because the pads of his fingertips felt so good.

He spread his hands across her waist and then her back as he kissed her. She held her breath. He was— she was—moving too fast. He trailed his fingers beneath her breasts, and even through her lacy bra, she felt his heat. She leaned into the pressure of his palms.

His thick laugh was all provocation. She reached between them and undid the button on the top of his jeans.

"You won't say 'oh no' again?" he asked.

Suddenly, she didn't mind feeling helpless. Aidan had the same problem.

"I'm staying awhile." Pain squeezed her heart. She kissed the stern line of Aidan's jaw. Tasting him, wanting him. "Eli hasn't changed. If he knew I cared about you, he'd still be upset."

"I need you. I think we can make things right." He pulled her shirt over her head. She froze, expecting to feel shy. Cool air kissed her skin, but yearning in Aidan's eyes made her hot. She reached behind her back and undid her bra. As it fell, she backed away. Aidan reached for her, but she turned toward the bedroom.

Aidan caught her at the door, dragging her hips

against him. His arousal pulsed at her back. Breathing hurt. He cupped her breasts, his hands tender, teasing.

She groaned and then felt the rumble of his voice against her throat. His pleasure deepened hers. His mouth followed the line of her shoulder, his patience both thrilling and frustrating her. At last, he turned her to face him and then he bent and closed his mouth around her nipple.

"Hold on to me," he whispered as the moisture from his mouth chilled her. He pushed her skirt off her hips and she stepped out of it.

"I'm nearly naked." In the grip of her body's need, she'd hardly noticed. "I don't know how you make me—no one else ever…" Admitting she'd never wanted anyone like this, even the father of her son, was too intimate. And too hard to take back.

"I'm glad." Aidan stared down her body, content to savor. She was not.

She unbuttoned his shirt and pushed it off his shoulders. Then she finished lowering his zipper. She slid her hand inside his jeans and stroked him. He inhaled, his fingers coming around her upper arms. Need begged in his guttural tone. His eyes never left hers as he covered her hand, urging her to caress him again.

As she did, he pushed his jeans down. She helped, kneeling to pull them off. When she stood, he was wearing only boxers, and she peeled off her panties.

She tossed them toward her skirt and turned back, to discover Aidan's boxers had joined his jeans.

Another moment of truth interrupted. If she didn't turn back this would be a memory all her life.

Did she prefer sweet memory or regret?

She reached for him, and he urged her toward the bed. She sat, only to pull him beside her. He slid his hand down her thigh, exciting her with his possessive touch. But she'd had enough foreplay after the drought of a long, lonely time. Unable to find words, uncertain that her bare basic need wouldn't turn him off, she tilted her head and kissed him—truly naked for the first time in her life.

"I hope you won't think I'm—" she whispered, spreading her legs.

"Beautiful? Passionate? Hungry for me? I'm thinking of how many years I wasted, not knowing you." He rolled above her, easing her legs farther apart, finding his way with his fingers first. "I don't think I can talk anymore."

"And I can't wait."

He eased inside her, his face tight, his eyes intense. Her body seemed to bloom. Desire, almost too acute, dragged his name out of her. His gaze was full of need. They found a rhythm as if making love were normal, not new and frantic.

Aidan leaned down again, kissing her breast, and she lost control. She closed her eyes as she abandoned herself to waves of pleasure, rousing only when he pulled away.

"No." She grabbed at his waist. He groaned and tried to hold himself away from her, but compulsion was too strong and he began to move again. With a strange, fierce grunt, he pulled out and collapsed against her. She was unprepared for the savagery of his kiss, like being marked.

With any other man she might have minded.

Later, he turned her face to his. "I'm sorry," he said. "We were both so fast, and I suddenly remembered we'd forgotten protection."

"No, you were right. The last thing… We shouldn't take a chance like that again."

"We won't." He kissed her as if they hadn't just made love, as if he wanted her again, and she could feel that he did.

"Wait here." He slid off the bed. In the faint light that came down the short hall from the living room, she watched him dress. "I'm not trying to be crude," he said. "I'd rather hold you right now and I want you to believe I can be romantic—but if I hold you in my bed, we're going to…"

"I'll wait."

"Will you be all right alone?"

"If you're not gone long."

"I'm asking if you're going to leave."

"No. I should, but I'll be here when you come back."

"I'm not a guy who does this and then leaves the next day." He pulled down the comforter and sheets and Beth slid beneath them, too wrung out to argue.

Aidan tucked the bedding around her, kissing her all the while. By the time he pulled away, she didn't want him to go, and he was reluctant. "This is what I meant," he said, cupping her breast through the sheet. "I need you."

"Then hurry."

He walked toward the door, trailing his hand down her stomach and her leg. When he reached the hall, his footsteps sped up. The door shut, and Beth pulled the sheets up to her shoulder, rolling over to burrow her face into the pillow.

She expected regret, but felt none. The house up the hill, empty and quiet, waited for her, but she'd rather be down here, sharing Aidan's bed.

He could talk all he wanted about who he was—who they both were—but she had other responsibilities. And the future no longer felt like a safe place.

CHAPTER THIRTEEN

BUYING "PROTECTION" after ten at night in Honesty, Virginia, drove the pimply faced boy behind the counter to offer a thumbs-up. Aidan took his package, turned down a bag for it and left the store.

He just hoped that kid didn't know Beth or Eli. With Eli on his mind, he gave the gas pedal an extra push.

What was he doing? He couldn't stay in Honesty, and Beth had said she wouldn't leave with him. Was he playing a game that would hurt her?

This didn't feel like a game. His need for her and his joy in her, had been powerful.

He'd made love with her. He had to have her again. He wasn't giving her up.

What about Eli? Beth was right. He needed more than another father figure who'd leave him. Aidan was already sure he couldn't stay away from Beth, but before Eli came home, he had to be able to tell her these feelings wouldn't change.

He ran into the cottage, shutting the door and locking it behind him. Neither of them would leave again tonight. He kicked off his shoes and padded through the house, unbuttoning his shirt.

Beth lay on her side, her eyes closed. Moonlight made her face pale against the pillow. Aidan set the box on the nightstand and finished undressing before he pushed the sheets down and slipped in beside her.

She turned to him, her arms opening.

"I thought you were asleep," he said.

"Mmm-hmm." Her mouth trailed across his chest, pausing to open, closing and bringing him delight.

"I like the way you sleep."

"Did you find what you were looking for?"

Her nails slid down his back, whisper-soft, causing sharp chills. He cupped her bottom and pulled her closer. She stopped, apparently startled that she could make him want her so badly, so soon.

"I can wait," she said, "but you go ahead."

"I'd hate to rush you."

"Like before?"

"You were rushed?"

"You were perfect."

"Not exactly," he said, "but this time…"

He turned over, pulling her across his body and she raised up, scooping her hair over her shoulders. Taking her breast in his mouth, he pushed her legs wider apart. She backed up, but he pulled her to him again, sliding his hands between them.

This time was different. Slower. And better.

IN THE MORNING, Aidan woke alone in a rumpled bed. He sat up, telling himself he'd lost her if she'd gone home. "Beth?"

She didn't answer, but he heard her voice, faint, yet full of false calm. He already knew her well enough to sense when she was pretending.

Pulling on his boxers, he followed her voice to the kitchen. She turned, wearing his shirt. "Eli?" he asked, plucking at the collar.

She lifted her hand. He couldn't tell what that meant, but he started coffee while she spoke into the phone.

"You're sure he slept well?" She waited. "And I still can't see him?" Another silence. "Two weeks is so long, Dr. Cook." Silence again. "All right, but you can expect me to call again. No, I can't wait. I'm sorry, but I can't." She turned to Aidan, her expression forlorn. "I can't be the only parent calling."

Aidan wrapped an arm around her shoulders, which seemed small and fragile. She leaned against him.

"I suspected the other mothers and fathers would be burning up the phone lines, too. Thanks, Dr. Cook." She hung up. "They won't let me see him."

"But they told you he'd be better off if you waited until he settled in."

"I'm not better off. It's hard to just let go."

"He can probably say things to them that he wouldn't put into words for you."

She wrapped her arms around him. "Yeah."

"Any regrets, Beth?"

"Not about last night." She looked up. "But don't worry. I'm not confused about the terms."

"Don't try to make me angry so I'll go away. I was there. We never mentioned terms."

"I did. You didn't listen," she said.

Not listening. "A problem we both need to work on." He stepped away from her.

"Don't get upset." She wasn't faking the annoying calm tone now. "Your life is somewhere else. We both felt alone, though I can't imagine you lack for women wanting you. We took comfort from each other."

"I'm not suggesting a man should live and die by stereotypes," he said, "but aren't those supposed to be my lines? Only, I'm not saying them."

"As long as someone does." She shrugged, and her hair cascaded over the shoulder of his shirt. She looked soft and sexy as hell and he wanted her, not just because her body had become vital to his happiness, but to make her admit that one night would not be enough. "I'd better take a shower," she said. "Do you mind?"

Too ticked off to answer, he tilted his head toward the bathroom. She went down the hall, and he ached, needing her.

His head told him to give her room. The closeness they'd found last night was enough to scare any woman whose ex-husband had hurt her. She'd built natural defenses.

The shower started. He imagined her, standing

naked, his shirt at her feet as she adjusted the water temperature.

Damn it, there was one way to show her he wasn't the only one who felt too much to walk away.

He swore. She'd probably assume he was weak. He definitely didn't feel strong.

She jumped when he opened the glass door, and she started to say no, but he took off his boxers again, and she backed beneath the water.

He took that as an invitation, but when he climbed in, she climbed out. He swore again as the door snicked shut. What the hell now? He pressed his hands against the tiled walls and swallowed mouthful after mouthful of warm water.

The door opened again, and Beth stepped back in, slipping a condom on top of the shower wall.

"You're a nice surprise." Smiling, he pulled her into his arms and reached for the soap as he sat on the bench at the back of the cubicle.

He ran soap down the valley between her breasts, kissing one nipple as he soaped her waist. She stretched in his arms, moaning her satisfaction as he touched her everywhere she liked best.

Finally, she took the soap and began to return the favor. After one night, she knew how to drive him crazy. He was clutching the walls on both sides of him, when she started to straddle him.

She stopped and reached for the condom. She put it on him, and he writhed, barely able to wait. At last he lifted her onto himself, and they both sighed, wrapping their arms around each other.

He had to slow her down, but she didn't seem to mind, leaning back, opening her body to his hands and mouth. He held her by the waist and lifted her.

"You could walk away from me?" he asked.

She breathed deep, and he had to let her down. They both groaned.

"Could you, Beth?"

"Right this minute?" She caught his hands, but he freed them and lifted her again. "No," she said.

"You want me to stop?"

"I want you to let me not stop." She traced his straining muscles with her fingertips.

"You're playing tough again this morning. I want you to be honest." Once more, he let her slide down. Holding on to his waist, she writhed in a way that made him gasp.

"You be honest," she said on half a breath.

"I honestly can't let you go," he said. "And I don't want to sneak around."

"We're not dating, Aidan. You've saved my family from a series of escalating crises." She rose and sank again. His legs trembled. Her eyes seemed to darken. Impossibly. "And you need to shut up."

She left him no choice.

AFTERWARD, they staggered back to his bed and slept in each other's arms. Beth woke, her first thought, anxiety for Eli, her second, wonder at the rightness of Aidan's arms around her.

Then she remembered Lucy, no doubt starving and dying to go out. She slid out of bed and called Mrs. Carlton who'd already taken care of the dog.

Afterward Beth hesitated beside the bed. She should go home. Aidan hadn't been swept off his feet by unexpected love. She still believed in the possibility of happily ever after, but she knew reality from a castle in the air. Love at first sight didn't happen between a man who owned more than his share of the world and a woman like her, who had a troubled son, too much debt and, at the moment, no place to call home.

Aidan didn't live like other men with his assets. The thought niggled, trying to offer her hope.

"What's on your mind?" he asked, patting the sheet. She lay back down, staring at the lightly tanned chest in front of her, noting each black hair. The bliss of his skin against hers. All temporary, like last night and this morning, each moment she'd share with him like this. It couldn't be permanent.

"Beth?"

"You're on my mind."

"What about me?"

"I wonder why you're—no, why I'm here. This is your place."

"Because you went for a walk and I waited, hoping you'd show up. Because I care about you, and you care, too."

Cared too much. She had her son. He had his grief to recover from. "Did you love Madeline?"

His body went rigid. "Where did that come from?"

"I wondered. She's on my mind a lot, too." Why wouldn't he relax into her arms again? How did Madeline still do that to him?

"Do we really want to talk about her right now?"

"What do you mean?" she asked, warily.

"When I'm making love to you, I'd rather not talk about my former wife."

That shook her.

"Do you feel guilty?" She sat up, tucking the sheet around her breasts. "Are you still in love with her? I worried about you feeling guilty, but I didn't think of that. Why are you in bed with me?"

His dark eyes glowed with satisfaction. "I'm in bed with you because I don't want to be anywhere else." His mouth, in a slow curve, made her want to sink against him. "My feelings for Madeline are complicated," he said. "Would you believe me if I said they weren't? But I didn't think of her as a wife for a long time before she died. I tried to. I wanted to, but I spent so much time trying to protect her that our marriage changed for me."

"That's not specific. Do you still love her?"

"Are you jealous?"

"Worse than that," she said. "Afraid. You're not over her."

"I am." But he looked uncertain. "I saw a therapist for several months, and he said I should move on. Use my name to do something for people who suffer from depression."

"You haven't. I would have heard."

"No, you wouldn't. I'm not some teenage girl with a dog in my purse." As she stared, he shrugged. "I'm not as interesting, but I've spoken to a medical group at home about building a center that offers the kind of care Eli's getting." He stopped, looking self-conscious. "For people who can't afford to go away. At the worst, this would make it easier for their families to visit. At best they'd be outpa—"

"No." Beth took the sheet with her as she stood. She found her shirt and underwear.

"Yes." He propped himself on his elbows, slightly amused, and not as concerned as she about being nude. "I've been there. I know it's moving forward."

She leaned down to put on her panties. "I'm glad you're helping, but I asked you about your feelings, and you switched to something you're doing. When it comes to how you feel, you try not to answer."

"Feelings." He might have been swearing. "How can you doubt what I feel after last night?"

"That's sex. It's like wanting food. Or water." Straightening, she flung her hair back. "Or absolution. Eli and I don't need you to build a little health center for us in my brother's cottage." She looked for her skirt, found it in the doorway and scrambled into it. "I'm getting out of here. Why wasn't I thinking? I'll get all attached to you. Eli already is, but you're looking to cleanse your soul. I will never understand men. You all fool me."

"You're jumping to the wrong conclusions because I can't find exactly the words you want."

"It's the only explanation," she said.

"For what?"

"We liked each other on sight. We're drawn to each other sexually. You found a couple of wounded creatures you could heal, and meanwhile, Madeline is still in your heart."

"Heal?" He touched his chest. "Look at me. I'm the one who's healing." His eyes widened. "I forgot to be afraid I'd die."

"Oh, my—" She caught her zipper on the hem of her shirt and tried to pull the zip back down. "Thank God, I didn't think of it, either."

"I mean, why would I be arrogant enough to think I could save anyone?"

"Because you lost your wife." She jerked at her zipper and then her shirt and then let both go. "You're trying to keep Eli and me alive as some sort of penance to her."

"Wait." He moved to the end of the bed, his eyes searching hers.

"I'm overreacting," she said, "because I've just spent the night with you, and I don't do that often, but you are still wrapped up in Madeline. You hardly say her name, and when I do you can't talk about her."

"Beth, you know me. I'm not just some guy." He

grabbed the sheet and wrapped it around his waist. "I've admitted you and Eli felt like my chance to make up for Madeline, but everything changed the second I saw Eli in the woods. With Madeline I knew I was too late. I was—you can't imagine." Beth flinched because he still felt so much. "But I got mad at Eli," he said. "I decided he wasn't going to die. I hope he understands how fragile life is, that he has only finite moments allotted to him, because I learned it in a flash, looking down at him on the ground."

"You're killing me. I don't want you ever to feel pain, but how did you make Madeline believe you loved her?"

He licked his lower lip and she wanted to sit down on the floor and cry. "I would have said anything to save her," he said. "I couldn't find the right words to make her believe, so I made some up—and that didn't work, either."

She exhaled as if he'd punched her in the stomach.

"You aren't like her, Beth. You're strong, and I don't lie to you. You can't trust that I'll never hurt you because people do that accidentally, but you can count on the truth from me."

"I lie, but never to you? That's believable."

"You're looking for reasons to go."

Even if he was right, it didn't matter. Her gut told her to run. She departed Aidan's bedroom and his house, but she was too late to escape.

He already owned too much of her heart.

SINCE HE HADN'T DIED saving Eli or losing Beth, Aidan stopped taking life easy. He put in a fax machine and a small copier, which Van okayed. He even made a run into D.C. after office hours, where he picked up work and earned himself an affronted phone call from his parents the next day.

"Dad," he said, midlecture, "I like living out here." An hour and a half wasn't that bad a drive.

Unless a man were making it for a woman who invented reasons to avoid him. Beth wouldn't even answer the phone to ask him to stop calling.

"What are you talking about, son?"

"He's trying to divert us," his mother said. "Pretending he wants to quit the company and move to the country to molder away at forty-two."

"I'm talking about an office in Honesty," Aidan said. "Maybe even in my home if I build one."

"Uh-huh? When I look out my window and see you zipping by on a flying monkey, I'll believe it." His mother took a deep breath that nearly blew out Aidan's eardrum. "If you're well enough to work, ask for what you need and we'll send it. Don't try to shock us into shutting up with threats of quitting or moving."

It didn't matter. Beth didn't want him. Eli had told him to go away.

He drove down the road to the fishing lodge a night or two during the next two weeks. The roof had gone up with lightning speed, as had the Sheetrock. On a Thursday at about ten at night, he saw

Beth in a white tank top, her hair curling around her shoulders, taping and spackling the drywall.

She tilted her head, evidently blowing her hair out of her face. Strands of it caught rays from the work light that hung on a hook above her head.

She looked good enough to—beg.

He backed down the driveway and out to the anonymous darkness of the main road, afraid he'd give in to temptation and fall on his knees at her feet.

He pulled out his cell phone and left a message at his cardiologist's office. "I'm through playing around. I'm going back to work, and if you don't want another patient, you should call my mother and let her know you're available if she needs you after I show up."

Next, he dialed Van's number. Van actually picked up.

"Aidan, are you calling for Beth? Has something happened to Eli?"

"He's fine as far as I know." Aidan's voice jumped as the car bumped over a pothole he couldn't miss.

"How about you?"

This family. They saw him as an invalid with a weak mind. "Fine, Van. I just wanted to let you know I'm going to start moving back to D.C."

"Already? You're welcome to the cottage for as long as you want it."

"I appreciate that, but I need to work again." Then he thought of actually leaving Beth and Eli.

He didn't want to. "I'll take my things back gradually. I'll still be in and out." Having made love to Van's sister all night long with more pleasure and hope than he'd felt in his adult life, he felt uncomfortable with her brother. "So, I'll talk to you whenever I'm back if you're around."

"Great. We should meet next time I'm in D.C. Catch a Nationals game."

"Sounds good."

It was all bland. Talk and times he'd share with clients and colleagues. He wanted more and he wanted it with this man's sister. "Talk to you later, Van."

Van needed no further prompting to hang up, and Aidan envied the other guy his busy schedule.

He tried Beth's number one last time. It rang and rang and rang three more times. Then there was a click and a second one. She'd answered and hung up. She didn't even want him in her voice mail.

IF THE CELL PHONE weren't her only tie to Eli, she'd have thrown the thing into that still cold lake. Beth wiped sweat off her forehead with the back of her wrist and slipped the cell back into her pocket.

Her jeans were fitting looser. Worry and work, an unbeatable diet, but not one she'd recommend.

In the past two weeks, she'd prepared almost every inch of the lodge for painting. As soon as the crew put up two pieces of drywall, she'd taped and slathered on spackling. Then came the sanding.

After the first hour of doing it by hand, she'd rented an electrical sander.

Each night, a couple of the drywall crew stayed behind to help. She donated beer and pizza and gratitude.

And she wished that just one of them would make her feel the slightest hint of interest. All tough, hard, good-looking guys, they were just friends. Her only interest was in Aidan, who'd invaded her dreams day and night.

When the phone rang again, she almost didn't look at it. She didn't trust herself to talk to Aidan. But she had to check the caller ID.

Her knees buckled when she read the camp's name.

She punched the Talk button. "Yes?"

"Mom?"

"Eli, are you crying?" She pressed her hand to the wall and smeared her palm in spackling. Eli's name repeated in her head. She couldn't get to him.

"I'm not crying. I'm yawning."

"Good try, buddy, but that doesn't even work when you're home. You're still a man if you cry. No matter what your dad says."

"Okay, I'm crying, but I have a good reason. You have to listen to me."

"I am." If she expected him to make changes, she had to as well. Campbell was a lousy father. She couldn't change that, but she could stop being an overprotective, neurotic attempt at two parents for the price of one. She stood still when what she really wanted was to run to her son. "Tell me."

"I think I—" He broke off, and then started again. But he was crying, sobbing.

"I can't understand you, honey."

He tried again, to no avail.

"Eli, I'll come. I'm on my way."

"No." It must have been a magical threat because he pulled himself together. "I've been talking to the doctor here, and I told him something I couldn't even tell Maria."

"But you need to tell me?"

"I'm trying."

She pressed her hand to her mouth.

"I think I burned down our house. I tried a cigarette, and it made me throw up. When I came back from the bathroom, my room was on fire, and I couldn't find the cigarette."

She couldn't believe what she was hearing. "You're wrong, sweetie. You're the victim of some horrible coincidence. Lightning literally struck when you did something you shouldn't. The firemen told me, and they can tell the difference." Poor guy. "This has been torturing you. It's why you wouldn't come to the lodge with me."

"I left the cigarette. I burned the house."

"No." She didn't know whether to laugh with joy that he'd finally told her something so painful or cry because he'd suffered for nothing. "If it had started with a cigarette, they'd know. Apparently, there are burn patterns, and our fire burned like a lightning strike."

She expected him to be relieved, too. He didn't say anything. She couldn't hear him breathing any more.

"Eli?"

"I don't know whether to believe you. Are you saying that because you're afraid I'll try to do that thing I did again?"

"I'm telling you the truth. You never had to worry about this. I just wish you could have told me."

"That I ruined our life? I was afraid you'd start acting like Dad. Who would I have left?"

"I've tried not to say anything bad about your father, but you have to know one thing through and through. I'm nothing like him. If you need me, I'll be there. You couldn't do anything to make me leave you. If I'm still around when we're both old and infirm, you'll still be giving me that tired 'Mom' that means you wish I'd leave you breathing space."

He laughed, but still with tears in his voice. "Okay."

"Really okay?"

"I'm trying."

Would he ever sound like a child again? "I love you, Eli."

"I'm glad I didn't burn down the house."

"Me, too, 'cause when you come home, you'll have no excuse to avoid helping me paint."

CHAPTER FOURTEEN

TWO WEEKS AFTER he left, Beth returned from her visit to Eli, singing. She parked in Van's garage, noted her brother's car with surprise, and climbed out of her own, balancing a wooden salad bowl Eli had made for her. By the time he came home, he planned to finish a set of six smaller bowls.

A man appeared in the garage door. With the last of the day's sunlight at his back, he was only a long, tall shadow.

Beth gasped.

"It's me," Aidan said. "Sorry for scaring you."

"I think Van's in the house."

"Don't pretend I'm here to see him."

"I'm sorry I ran out like that," she said, facing him at last. "But it's not just that Madeline's on your conscience. You can't even talk about her, and I'm afraid you still love her. I can't stand to be around you thinking that."

"It's ridiculous, Beth." He lifted one hand, to stop her from arguing. "Were you just visiting Eli?"

"He's better. It turns out he thought he'd set the

fire at our house. After he told me that, Dr. Cook said he started improving."

"Did he start the fire?"

"Not according to the firemen." She nudged the car door shut with her hip. "Not that I'll be asking them to take a second look. He tried a cigarette to get back at me."

"For what?"

"Being such a wet blanket," she said. "So I'm trying to change."

"But not with me?"

She couldn't think of anything she'd rather do than make a happy, healthy life with Aidan. "You aren't over her."

"I told you everything changed when I found Eli. I wanted him to be safe. I didn't help him because I thought he was Madeline. I wanted *him* to be safe. Your son—who matters to me, too.

She pressed her hand to her stomach. The words were exactly what she wanted to hear, but too late. "He doesn't want you in our lives."

"He told you that?"

"He told you."

"He was upset that day. Let me try again with him."

"I'm trying to see myself clearly because I tend to want things my own way, and I have too much pride, but this is about you. Until you're over your past, you can't ask me or Eli to think of you as part of our family."

He flinched. Then he turned and walked out of the garage, down the hill. She found it harder to stay put this time. She wanted to run after him and say it didn't matter that he couldn't talk about his ex-wife.

Except it did.

"How's Eli?" Van handed her a beer as she set her stuff on the kitchen counter.

"Good. He's bruised and he scratched his face on a rock, but he smiled—I don't know how many times—and he organized a poker game. With cards," she said. "It wasn't on a computer screen or a portable game player."

"Did he take your money?"

"Crackers. They're not allowed to play for money." She put the beer back and got water. Her chat with Aidan had left her throat dry. "Thank goodness. I'd have had to mortgage the car to get home. It's burning oil."

"I'll look at it tomorrow." He sipped his beer. "Was that Aidan outside?"

"Don't bother with the careful tone. I'm not seeing him anymore."

"But you were? I thought so in the hospital."

"I thought he cared for me."

"I think he does, too." Van didn't sound as if he approved.

"He wanted to save someone. His wife is still on his mind."

"How?"

"He can't talk about her. It'd be different if she was like Campbell—if he'd disliked her. But he loved her, and every time her name comes up, he changes the subject."

"How does he say he feels?"

Beth's skin went hot from her throat all the way up.

"You really care about him?" Van asked.

Just like that, "I love him" ran through her mind. "Eli liked him until he realized something was going on between us."

"Eli needs a dad."

"You think that's what he liked about Aidan?"

"That and the hero act."

"It was no act. He helped Lucy and Eli would have died without him."

He smiled. "You're arguing on his behalf."

"Cunning of you to trick me." She drank long and deep of her water. "I make mistakes, too, but Madeline's on his mind, and Eli's fragile. I can't ask him to consider Aidan as—anything—only to have him leave."

Van considered his answer. Finally, he shrugged in surrender. "What are we doing for dinner?"

"Wishing Mrs. Carleton lived here full time." Beth opened the fridge. "She usually leaves some-thing for me." Sure enough, a plate of sandwiches nestled in plastic wrap. "I would marry her," she said. "She thinks of everything and she wouldn't know how to shade the truth if you gave her directions."

"You're calling Aidan a liar? Not even his worst business adversaries accuse him of lying."

"I don't mean that. I just can't know how he really feels, and he acts as if Madeline still matters." She braced her hands on her hips, no longer feeling strong, so she tried to look it. "I'm not hungry. I'm going to have a shower."

"I saw him loading his car when I got home. He's started moving his things back to D.C."

Beth turned to the nearest window that overlooked the cottage. Breathing suddenly took all her energy. She had to will her feet to the floor, or she'd have run down the hill.

And say what?

"Don't go. I love you. I don't care that my son resents you. I'm not really afraid because I care this much about a man I've only known a month. I'm not positive you still love Madeline."

"Beth?" Van said, "You're from different worlds. He's always chased business. He has a tragic past that colors the way he looks at you and Eli. You're happy in naive little Honesty, and he travels more than he's home."

"See? You've thought of more reasons than I did."

He nodded. "But maybe you're more distrustful of Aidan than you should be. I love Eli as if he were my own, but I can see he'll learn to love Aidan because Aidan won't let him down."

"You're arguing for him now?"

"I'm suggesting you don't let him go without talking to him about what you really want."

"We've said it all. He's building a home for people with trouble like Madeline's. His therapist told him to do it for his health's sake. And I think, instinctively, he wanted to build another little home here. Dragging Eli and me back from that tree with the broken branch signed the dotted line on his bill of good health."

"He told you that?"

"He didn't have to. He thrives on good works, and Eli and I needed a few."

"What if all your worst fears and mine are true, but he's a nice guy, and he honestly cares for you and Eli?"

"What if time goes by and he learns to live with what happened—while he's living with Eli and me. He cares about us—fine, but one day, a woman walks into his office or bumps into him at the lodge—and he falls in love. Truly in love—she's not a Band-Aid over the past."

"Have a little faith in yourself. You're no one's idea of a Band-Aid."

AIDAN HAD TWO THINGS to do on his last day in Honesty. First he had to thank Van for the cottage and second, he had to deliver a fishing pole he'd ordered for Eli.

It sat beside his laptop case, but he kept circling

it. He'd ordered it the first night he went to the lodge, coming home with that glittering lake on his mind. He'd seen himself and Eli fishing off the deck, as he'd done with his grandfather.

Eli would prefer a skateboard. Aidan should toss the fishing pole or better yet, donate it to Goodwill. Maybe he'd ask Van to.

Just as well Beth's car wasn't in the garage when he walked up to the house.

Van came out. "They're at the lodge."

"I came to say thanks." Two months had passed since he'd come to Honesty. He could have gone home, back to work, at least a month ago. Instead, he'd kept returning to Honesty and the people he loved most.

He wasn't using Beth to bind his own wounds.

"You're welcome." Van shook his hand. "Use it any time. Nice pole. Is that for Eli?"

"Yeah, but I think he'd rather have a skateboard."

"I ordered that kit he wants," Van said. "But he likes to fish, too. His pole burned in the fire."

"He had one?"

"Living a few hundred feet from that lake? He learned to fish before he could walk."

"Would you give it to him? Tell him I'm sorry I missed him."

"The lodge is on your way out of town."

"The last time I saw Eli he told me to leave."

"He's better," Van said. "Not well yet, but better. Give him a chance to apologize."

"He doesn't have to." Aidan set the fishing pole against the porch rail.

Van picked it up. He tilted the box as if he were aiming a gun, making a big deal of reading the small print. "My sister's been sad."

"She'll be better when Eli is."

"That's the funny thing. That trip up to the mountains helped Eli, but Beth looks as if her life has gone wrong. And usually she's looking toward the cottage when I think that."

"She doesn't believe me."

"She'll kill me for doing this, but stop by the lodge. Talk to them." Van held out the pole.

Aidan hesitated. How many times had he run to her rescue like the nut she apparently thought he was? Shouldn't he get out of her life and assume he'd learn to care for someone else?

"If I loved a woman, I wouldn't wait for everything to be right. I'd take action."

Aidan had just about had it with this family. Unless he was mistaken, Van had just called him a lazy coward, and Beth, whom he loved with everything that was best in him, assumed taking care of her was an act to ease his conscience, and that he really loved his former wife.

He took the fishing pole, listing overnight delivery services in his head.

"See you around," he said. "Thanks again for everything."

"Maybe I went one piece of advice too far." Van

stepped back, shoving his hands in his pockets. "Have Beth call me if they're not coming home for dinner. Mrs. Carleton hates cooking for three if she only has to feed one."

Aidan had no laugh to spare for a Mrs. Carleton joke. He walked down the hill, tossed the pole on top of his laptop in the car's back seat and went back to lock the cottage door and drop the key in the letter box.

Driving through Honesty, he was surprised by a feeling of wistfulness. The trees had filled out so that many of the shop roofs were hard to see.

Trey Lockwood nodded at him, exiting the hardware store with a length of chain in his hands. A couple more of Beth's friends nodded as Aidan drove by.

He passed the park. The memory of Beth standing at the picket fence, and then lying beneath him in his bed later that night nearly choked him. Memories too sweet to be real. Need and passion too mutual and potent to ignore.

He tried. How many times could he beg Beth to turn him down? He saw the lodge road and told himself to drive by. Drive on by.

At the last minute, his hands turned the wheel. The car skidded into her lane. Swearing, he kept going. He didn't know when to shut up and go home.

He met Eli on the road. The boy, splattered with paint, was trying to ride a skateboard in the grass. It stuck so suddenly, he fell over.

Aidan stopped and let down his window. Only Beth's car sat in front of the house. Eli glanced back at it. Then he stood, dusting off his jeans.

"I'm fine," he said.

Still mad. "How's Lucy?"

"Fine. She's in the woods, chasing things. She won't get hurt here." Where Aidan didn't belong.

"I have something for you."

Eli brightened. "Are you leaving?"

"It's more than time." He'd hoped Eli might have been annoyed in the hospital because he didn't want any guy around after Campbell, but treatment hadn't changed anything. Aidan got out and opened the back door.

Eli stayed where he was. Inwardly, Aidan sighed. No indignity too large. He carried the fishing rod into the grass. To his surprise, Eli's mouth formed an O when he held out the pole.

"That's top of the line. I can't take that."

"I ordered it before you were angry with me. My grandfather gave me one like it when I was your age."

"You fish?" Eli unbent.

"When I get the chance." Aidan offered the pole again. "Not often in the past few years."

"That's how my mom would have to live if she liked you."

"What?"

"She'd have to give up stuff she likes. Living here, canoeing on the lake. Friends, Uncle Van."

"I care about her, Eli."

"So did my dad."

That tore it. "I'm not like him. I'd never ask your mom to give up anything." He got down to what he suspected Eli really feared. "Just like I'd never ask you to. I live in D.C. I'm just getting to know you and your mother, and I like you both. It doesn't mean I'd ask you to move to Washington."

"But eventually… And then, when you got tired of us, there we'd be, stuck."

"I don't get tired easy," Aidan said. "And I know how much you like being with your friends. I don't think I'm more important than you."

"My dad does. Is he so different from other guys?"

"He's different from me."

Eli stared at him, torn between taking up for his father, and the sad truth he'd so recently learned. Finally, he took the fishing pole. "Thanks. My mom may make me give it back."

"I'll tell her I want you to have it."

"Eli?"

Aidan looked toward the house, happy at the sound of Beth's voice.

"How much do you like her?" Eli asked.

"This is a funny conversation to have with a young man your age." Eli stopped looking young. The old man who'd looked out of his eyes during that first week came back. "I love her," Aidan said.

Eli froze.

"It's the truth," Aidan said, "and it's what I'm going to tell your mother. I want you to be my family."

He turned his head and shaded his eyes against the sun. Beth looked back, also beneath the shade of her hand. Aidan started up the hill.

Beth came down to meet him, as if she didn't want him in the house taking shape behind her. "Where's Eli going?"

"I brought him a fishing rod." As they watched he walked down to the dock. Without looking back.

"What did you say to him? Is he upset?"

"I told him I love you."

"What?" He might have suggested she leap off that dock.

"Not what you wanted to hear?" he asked.

"Why would you—"

"Someone suggested I take action." He took her hand. "Do you want to go inside?"

"I don't ever want to remember you inside my house."

"Because I matter to you," he said. "I'm in the same sad shape where you two are concerned. Only I'm willing to take the chance. I believe we can love each other and no one will get hurt."

"I'm not worried about—"

"You are," he said, realizing it had to be true even as he spoke. "I thought you were the bravest woman I knew because you could laugh even when things went bad. I went out of my way to show you how I felt. I had to be a stalker or a man in love. But you used to believe Campbell, who lied to you, so you'd rather think I'm a nut trying to heal my former wife."

"That's almost too much sweet talk, Aidan. Notice, I can stand it if you say my ex's name."

"Why don't we stop talking?" He put his arms around her, forgetting Eli, forgetting fear, knowing only that being with Beth made him live again.

"Eli…" she said.

"Better get used to seeing you in my arms." He kissed her, gently at first, when he wanted to roll over her defenses.

She held on to his arms and tried to lean back, but her lips softened. She slanted her mouth against his, reaching for his shoulders, pulling closer.

"Wait. What about Madeline? Are you sure this isn't—"

"Talking about my first wife with you makes me feel odd." He stepped back, wiping his mouth. "I love you more, need you more and I won't give up. I tried to love her. I can't stop loving you."

"What if you get tired of me? I'm no judge of men."

"What is it with you and Eli? I won't get tired of you."

"What about him? He could get sick again. He's not entirely better yet."

"We'd get him help again. He'd be my son, too." He looked toward the lake, where Eli was wrestling with the pieces of his new fishing pole. "I'd be proud to call him my son."

"But Campbell—"

"Is a waste of breath. I want to love you and your son. And all I ask is that you take me on, too."

"I want more children," she said.

"Keep throwing obstacles at me," he said. "I'd be happy if we had to build the house all the way to the lake to fit us all in."

"Is it this easy? Talking about our differences and finding common ground?"

"No," he said. "We can talk forever, but you and Eli have to take a leap of faith. I did that the night Eli lived. You can't wait for someone to nearly die because I'll be really pissed if any one of us is in that much danger again."

"I have to be certain."

"No one gets to be as sure as you want to be," he said. "You have to decide."

She grabbed a loop of her wavy hair and tugged.

"You're weighing the pros and cons," he said. "I wish I could laugh."

He started down the hill, a city boy who might tumble ass over teakettle with the next step. Maybe she was giving him a lucky out.

"Wait."

He stopped.

She ran down the hill, grabbing him so hard he almost fell and dragged her with him. "I'm scared of a lot of things, but most of all, I'm scared of losing you."

She looped her arm around his neck and this time

she kissed him, opening his mouth with hers, taking him back to the thick, silent moments of need in his bedroom. She pushed her hand to his cheek.

"You're mine," she said. "I'll risk everything, but I won't let you go if you stay now. You're stuck with us forever, and when things go wrong, you'll just have to fight with me until everything's right again."

"That's life, Beth. That's how two people who love each other live together."

"Forever," she said again, as if he didn't want it.

"I guess you two do like each other." Bound up in fishing line, Eli looked like a piece of living string art.

What had he seen? What had he heard? "I meant everything." Aidan pulled Beth against his side. "You're both my future if you'll have me."

"Do you mind us being together?" Beth asked. "Did you dislike Aidan or are you reluctant to have any guy give us more grief?"

"Like Dad." Eli straightened, and the fishing line glittered in bright sunlight. "I won't put up with that, Aidan."

"Then you'll have to put up with the best life I can give you."

"You'll have to try, too, Eli," Beth said. "None of us compromises easily."

"Way to make love sound like work, Mom." Eli whistled for Lucy and started back to the lake, yanking at fishing cord that tightened around various body parts. "I don't know why you two even care what a kid thinks anyway."

"Are you okay?" Aidan called.

"Yeah, I'm okay with it." Lucy bolted out of the trees and ran him down. They rolled down the hill, boy and dog and fishing wire a single package.

Aidan and Beth ran to sort them out—holding hands, so that when they fell, too, they rolled into Eli and Lucy and formed a laughing ball of string and loving family.

EPILOGUE

"I'M JUST SAYING we could have made a crapload of money during a four-day holiday, Mom."

Up to her elbows in turkey and the hope of producing an edible dinner, Beth turned to her son. "While I'm always interested in a 'crapload' of anything," she said, "being just the three of us for our first Thanksgiving mattered more to Aidan and me."

"Uncle Van's coming."

"He's family, too."

"All right. We have bills to pay, but I guess you guys are running the show."

"Yes, we are." And thank goodness it was all right with him. She and Aidan were a little happier every time he handed over control and adult worries about their home to the real grown-ups.

"I'm going to see if Jeff's outside. I called about a half hour ago and his mom was making him peel yams." He hurried down the hall.

"Hey—can moms do that? I have some yams."

"See ya later." The closet door opened. Something thudded into a wall, and then something else scraped the still-new paint job. "It's okay. I'll clean it up," Eli said. "Bye."

The front door opened and then slammed shut.

Beth laughed out loud. Sometimes a woman had to love life. Then she caught a glimpse of the dressing, which seemed to expand every time she turned her back on it. How did that whole pile of revolting stuff get inside the turkey and cook? Aidan and his big talk of loving a traditional meal.

"Need an extra pair of hands?"

The turkey slipped into the sink. "I thought you were testing office connections," Beth said. Aidan's new home office sat closer to the lake. Every time she visited and stared out his wall of windows onto the water, she was tempted to displace him.

"It's all working. I thought you might like some help." He leaned over her shoulder, but drew back. "Are you sure that's—"

"As good as a dinner reservation? No." She plunged her hands in again. "If you could wash up and steady this bird…"

"You plan to feed this to our family?"

"If Eli didn't look too closely, and you don't tell Van how it looks right now. Think of it as practice for when your parents come at Christmas." She spooned some of the stuffing in and caught the turkey before it slipped again. Then she caught his smirk. "Don't go all moral on me. It's your duty, Aidan." She lifted her face for his kiss. He laughed as he took advantage of her busy hands and her defenseless body.

Sighing, she swayed against him. "Help me get this in the oven and we can close our bedroom door for a little while."

"I never thought I'd hear you ask for help without trying everything on your own first." He bundled the turkey into its roasting pan and then into the oven.

Beth stared wistfully through the window set in the door. "I won't be able to let you help at Christmas. That is going to be one ugly Thanksgiving bird."

"I'll take your mind off it."

Several hours later, Beth shooed Van and Eli to the dining table where her mother's china gleamed beneath candlesticks Aidan's parents had sent as a housewarming gift. Aidan lit the candles and took his place at the head of the table. Van and Eli wrestled to their places on opposite sides.

"Van," Beth said.

"You're too serious."

Aidan's smile took her to the less serious two hours they'd shared that afternoon. She grinned.

"It's a moment to be serious." Aidan cleared his throat, but laughed anyway and Van and Eli laughed, too, though they didn't know why. Beth felt herself blushing. Secure in her lover's heart, she didn't feel vulnerable any more.

"What's up, Mom?"

"Nothing. Where's Lucy?"

"I couldn't find her." Just a few months ago, he'd have been frantic. Now he was able to leave Lucy to her doggie concerns. "What were you and Aidan laughing about?"

"Private joke," Van said.

"Oh." He looked from Aidan to his mother, who went blank instead of coming up with a pithy distraction. "Gross."

"Van," Beth said again.

"Let me in here," Aidan said. "I'm trying to toast my new family."

"Let's toast." Van lifted his glass.

"Mom," Eli did likewise, "can I have a sip of wine, too?"

"No." She still overprotected her son at moments she found as startling as he. He was better. He no longer took antidepressants and he only visited his therapist once every two weeks. But she wasn't about to add even a teaspoon of wine to the mix.

"I'm fine, Mom."

"I know." She put all her love in the smile she shot him.

"Don't get all mushy." Eli lifted his water glass to Aidan. "Better get on with it. That turkey looks funny but I'm starving."

One of the wings had bent at an odd angle, and half the breast was a bit more well-done than its golden, glowing mate. No doubt due to distraction on the part of the cooks.

She sipped her wine.

"Beth," Aidan said. Van laughed and took a sip, too. Eli waved his water with so much enthusiasm several drops spilled on the tablecloth. A bargain find—not the one they'd be using at Christmas with the Nikolases.

"Sorry. I was thinking." Beth wiped her mouth. "Let's try again."

"I was going to say that no one had more reason to be thankful than I," Aidan said, "because I've found the woman I love and a boy I want to call my own son."

Beth stiffened. "You can't do that unless—"

"Let me ask you before you answer," Aidan said.

All the laughter stopped. Beth glanced at Eli, whose hope was intense. She looked at Van, who eyed her, worried.

"It's all right," she said. "We still have nothing in common, except I love him and he loves me and we count on each other, and Eli knows he can trust us both."

"You're not a novelty to him, are you?" Van asked.

"No," Aidan said, his tone dry. "In case you've both forgotten I'm here." He and Eli commiserated with a clink of their glasses. "She's the woman I'll love all my life. She's the woman I want for my wife."

"And she's saying yes," Beth said. "Yes and yes again. What do you think, Eli?"

Before he could answer, Lucy burst through the

dog flap, click-clacked down the hall, skidded into the door frame and then stared at the family around the table.

"Over here, girl." Eli pointed to a bone in her dish beside his chair.

"Beth, will you marry me?"

"And love you forever and ever and ever."

"Gross," Van and Eli said together.

Aidan came around the table. "Let's make it worse for them." Dipping her over one arm, he kissed her so thoroughly the chair rocked behind her. For a moment, she thought she should grab for it, but then she didn't care.

* * * * *

Turn the page for a sneak preview of
IF I'D NEVER KNOWN YOUR LOVE
by
Georgia Bockoven

From the brand-new series
Harlequin Everlasting Love
Every great love has a story to tell. ™

One year, five months and four days missing

There's no way for you to know this, Evan, but I haven't written to you for a few months. Actually, it's been almost a year. I had a hard time picking up a pen once more after we paid the second ransom and then received a letter saying it wasn't enough. I was so sure you were coming home that I took the kids along to Bogotá so they could fly home with you and me, something I swore I'd never do. I've fallen in love with Colombia and the people who've opened their hearts to me. But fear is a constant companion when I'm there. I won't ever expose our children to that kind of danger again.

I'm at a loss over what to do anymore, Evan. I've begged and pleaded and thrown temper tantrums with every official I can corner both here and at home. They've been incredibly tolerant and understanding, but in the end as ineffectual as the rest of us.

I try to imagine what your life is like now, what you do every day, what you're wearing, what you eat. I want to believe that the people who have you are misguided yet kind, that they treat you well. It's how I survive day to day. To think of you being mistreated hurts too much. If I picture you locked away somewhere and suffering, a weight descends on me that makes it almost impossible to get out of bed in the morning.

Your captors surely know you by now. They have to recognize what a good man you are. I imagine you working with their children, telling them that you have children, too, showing them the pictures you carry in your wallet. Can't the men who have you understand how much your children miss you? How can it not matter to them?

How can they keep you away from us all this time? Over and over, we've done what they asked. Are they oblivious to the depth of their cruelty? What kind of people are they that they don't care?

I used to keep a calendar beside our bed next to the peach rose you picked for me before you left. Every night I marked another day, counting how many you'd been gone. I don't do that any longer. I don't want to be reminded of all the days we'll never get back.

When I can't sleep at night, I tell you about

my day. I imagine you hearing me and smiling over the details that make up my life now. I never tell you how defeated I feel at moments or how hard I work to hide it from everyone for fear they will see it as a reason to stop believing you are coming home to us.

And I couldn't tell you about the lump I found in my breast and how difficult it was going through all the tests without you here to lean on. The lump was benign—the process reaching that diagnosis utterly terrifying. I couldn't stop thinking about what would happen to Shelly and Jason if something happened to me.

We need you to come home.

I'm worn down with missing you.

I'm going to read this tomorrow and will probably tear it up or burn it in the fireplace. I don't want you to get the idea I ever doubted what I was doing to free you or thought the work a burden. I would gladly spend the rest of my life at it, even if, in the end, we only had one day together.

You are my life, Evan.

I will love you forever.

* * * * *

*Don't miss this deeply moving Harlequin
Everlasting Love story about a woman's struggle
to bring back her kidnapped husband from
Colombia and her turmoil over whether to let go,
finally, and welcome another man into her life.
IF I'D NEVER KNOWN YOUR LOVE
by Georgia Bockoven
is available March 27, 2007.*

*And also look for
THE NIGHT WE MET
by Tara Taylor Quinn,
a story about finding love
when you least expect it.*

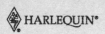

presents a brand-new trilogy by

PATRICIA THAYER

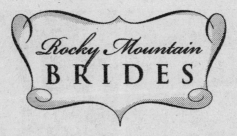

Rocky Mountain
BRIDES

Three sisters come home to wed.

In April don't miss
Raising the Rancher's Family,

followed by
The Sheriff's Pregnant Wife,

on sale May 2007,

and

A Mother for the Tycoon's Child,

on sale June 2007.

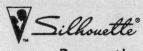

Silhouette®
Romantic
SUSPENSE

Excitement, danger and passion guaranteed!

USA TODAY bestselling author
Marie Ferrarella
is back with the second installment
in her popular miniseries,
*The Doctors Pulaski: Medicine
just got more interesting...*
DIAGNOSIS: DANGER is on sale
April 2007 from Silhouette®
Romantic Suspense (formerly
Silhouette Intimate Moments).

*Look for it wherever
you buy books!*

Silhouette Desire

Introducing talented new author

TESSA RADLEY

*making her Silhouette Desire debut
this April with*

BLACK WIDOW BRIDE

Book #1794
Available in April 2007.

Wealthy Damon Asteriades had no choice but to
force Rebecca Grainger back to his family's estate—
despite his vow to keep away from her seductive
charms. But being so close to the woman society once
dubbed the Black Widow Bride had him aching to
claim her as his own...at any cost.

On sale April from Silhouette Desire!

Available wherever books are sold,
including most bookstores, supermarkets,
discount stores and drugstores.

REQUEST YOUR FREE BOOKS!
2 FREE NOVELS PLUS 2 FREE GIFTS!

HARLEQUIN®

Super Romance®

Exciting, emotional, unexpected!

HSR07

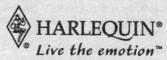

HARLEQUIN®

Super Romance®

COMING NEXT MONTH

#1410 ALL-AMERICAN FATHER • Anna DeStefano
Singles...with Kids

What's a single father to do when his twelve-year-old daughter is caught shoplifting a box of *expired* condoms? Derrick Cavennaugh sure doesn't know. He turns to Bailey Greenwood for help, but she's got troubles of her own....

#1411 EVERYTHING BUT THE BABY • Kathleen O'Brien

Having your fiancé do a runner is not the way any bride wants to spend her wedding day. Learning it's not the first time he's done it can give a woman a taste for revenge. And when a handsome man gives her the opportunity to do just that, who wouldn't take him up on it? Especially when it means spending more time with him.

#1412 REAL COWBOYS • Roz Denny Fox
Home on the Ranch

Kate Steele accepts a teaching job at a tiny school in rural Idaho. The widow of a rodeo star, she's determined to get her young son away from Texas and the influence of cowboys. Then she meets Ben Trueblood. He's the single father of one of her pupils—and a man she's determined to resist, no matter how attractive he is. Because he might call himself a buckaroo, but a cowboy by any other name...

#1413 RETURN TO TEXAS • Jean Brashear
Going Back

Once a half-wild boy fending for himself, Eli Wolverton is alive because Gabriela Navarro saved his life. They fell in love, yet Eli sent her away. Now she has returned to bury her father. He, like Eli's mother, died mysteriously in a fire—and Eli is accused of setting both. When Gaby and Eli meet again in the small Texas town they grew up in, one question is uppermost in her mind: is the boy she adored now the man she should fear...or the only man she will ever love?

#1414 MARRIED BY MISTAKE • Abby Gaines

Imagine being jilted on live TV in front of millions of people.... Well, that's not going to happen to this particular bride at Adam's TV station—not if he can help it by stepping into the runaway groom's shoes to save Casey Greene from public humiliation. Besides, it's not as if it's a real wedding. Right?

#1415 THE BABY WAIT • Cynthia Reese
Suddenly a Parent

Sarah Tennyson has it all planned out. In two months she'll travel to China to adopt her beautiful baby girl. But that's before everything goes awry. Apparently what they say is true...life *is* what happens when you're busy making plans.